...by daphne

Carmen Catalina

PublishAmerica
Baltimore

ISBN: 1-60813-125-4
PUBLISHED BY PUBLISHAMERICA, LLLP
www.publishamerica.com
Baltimore

Printed in the United States of America

For Mia, for my mom, Cynthia Miles, and the two who aren't here to see this: George Robert Thomas and George W. Miles.

To the O'Brien Library —
Stay positive and
follow your dreams!
♡ Carmen

1

Daphne sat at her desk and watched impatiently as the second hand slowly made its way around the clock. Tapping her fingers against her cheek, the last two minutes of eighth grade couldn't end fast enough. It had officially been the worst school year of her life. She watched the last fifteen seconds finish and was out of her seat before the bell sounded.

She heaved a huge sigh of relief as she walked amongst the kids in the corridor of her school. She watched as kids emptied their lockers and was glad that she had cleaned out her locker days before. She only had her backpack that carried a few knitting supplies and she held a green notebook that she considered her journal against her chest. She had to step over kids that were sitting on the floor, exchanging yearbooks to be signed. She'd bought one, but didn't dare ask anyone to sign it for fear that they wouldn't, and fear that they would. She was afraid they'd write "K.I.T." which they never really meant, and add their phone number which usually became disconnected. She wouldn't forget the phone numbers listed in her sixth grade memory book that she tried to call where the kids were either not home, walking the dog, taking a bath or away at camp.

But this year, well it was finally over. The pressure of school, and always looking around to see who might be staring at her, or making fun of her, was finally over.

She walked through the parking lot and along the sidewalk that was in front of the school, the warm June air caused sweat beads to form on her forehead. She watched school busses pass her and could hear the shuffle of sneakers against the hot cement behind her. Daphne lived only a few blocks away from school. She couldn't wait to get to her air conditioned room and take off her bulky sweater. She could feel sweat forming on her upper lip and tried to ignore it along with her forehead sweat, to take in the beauty of the day. The last day of school! The joy of it couldn't put a damper on the knowledge that as usual, she had no exciting summer plans. The long summer ahead, sitting in her room, working on knitting or scrap booking pictures she'd cut out of magazines of her favorite rock band Aquarium sounded glorious now that the worst school year of her life had finally come to an end. A school bus passed her and she heard someone shouting towards her.

"Have a fun summer pin cushion face!" a boy yelled out.

She looked up briefly to see Ty Stone hanging his head out of a window. She could see other kids snickering through the windows as the bus passed. She clutched her notebook to her chest tighter but the warmth of her own arms against her body didn't keep the tears from streaming down her face. She picked up her walking speed, but her pace was no match against the thoughts that raced through her mind. Ty Stone was a troublemaking, freckled faced boy who made her life a living hell. Pin cushion face? The nerve! He wasn't even remotely attractive and she knew in her heart that in fifteen years he'd probably be bald and fat! They didn't even have any classes together. Still, he'd made it a point, daily, to call her something terrible every time they passed in the hall. If it wasn't fatty, ugly, retard or brace face it was something else. Pin cushion face was a new one. It hurt her most of all knowing it was a reference to her complexion that broke out horribly a few months ago. Daphne went through tube after tube of Clearasil but it didn't seem to help, "clear" her face up.

Her pimples reminded her of her mom's gray hairs. Her mom Helen would stand in front of a mirror, holding tweezers while pulling out hairs Daphne couldn't even see and every time, every single time she'd say the same thing: "You know, every time you take out a gray hair seven more come back. It's why I have to do this every day, but I swear to you I will not dye my hair yet!"

Daphne didn't pop her pimples, yet every night before she went to bed with Clearasil slathered on her cheeks, she'd wake up to a few more. Her classmates at school acted as if they'd never seen anyone with breakouts before. Memories of walking into class and them asking her if she had the chicken pox while clucking chicken sounds will probably haunt her forever. The absolute horror of it was almost too much for her to bare. She'd never hurt anybody the way her classmates hurt her. She may have only been a teenager, but she already knew a thing or two about tact. Not to mention the embarrassment of it all. She'd been crushing on a hottie, Todd Newsome. There's nothing to help you get over a crush than having the class punk, Ty Stone cry out, "what the hell happened to you?" as she entered class one day. The class she also shared with Todd and she couldn't look at him the rest of the year. Todd was dreamy, with thick, curly hair and bright blue eyes he was the star of the basketball team. She'd go to the basketball games, and sit high in the bleachers where no one could see her, just to watch him play. She'd tell her mom it was school spirit, and it was never any problem for her to go because they lived so close. School spirit left her body exactly the way a balloon loses its air: fast and shrinking away to nothing, the way Ty embarrassed her in class that day. She never went to another basketball game after that, which was unfortunate to the team since she was one of only a handful of people who actually went.

Thank God for the real true love of her life, Posiadyn Fisher, the mysterious and sexy lead singer of Aquarium. Her heart beat for Posiadyn Fisher. Her future revolved around him. She had it all planned out, if only they could meet.

Once she reached the driveway to her house, she sighed, anticipation and dread all at once. She knew what lurked behind the front door. Toys from one end of the living room to the other, so many you couldn't walk without tossing them aside with your feet. Sometimes she would trip over the cords of their video games. Her seven year-old twin brothers, Ryan and Ritchie, would be perpetually sitting in front of the TV playing video games. They and their stuff were always everywhere or under her feet and she hated it. Without the sanctuary of her own room, she didn't know how she was able to live with those two slobs.

"Hey sis!" they yelled out to her as she entered.

"Hi" she said as she walked past them, trying to avoid their gaze so they couldn't tell she was crying, and up the stairs to her room.

Once inside her room she tossed her backpack on the bed, took off her sweatshirt in one full swoop and plopped down with a huge sigh. The sweat beads disappeared as soon as she entered the house and she was nice and cool. The tranquility of her room also eased her grief over the new name she'd been called on the way home.

How she loved her room! As she looked at all of her favorite things she didn't know what she wanted to do first to kick start her summer.

Daphne twisted her long, dark hair into a knot on top of her head and positioned some chopsticks through it. After she broke out, it was easier to hide by letting her hair hang in her face, so she stopped putting it up. But in the privacy of her room, where she could look in the mirror and put on her favorite lip gloss, she knew the truth of her beauty and felt no need to hide. What she saw when she looked in the mirror were sparkling brown eyes full of hope and dreams. She knew the promise of the braces was a beautiful smile, to go with her full lips. She couldn't wait to get the braces off, she was sure her smile would be so dazzling that Posiadyn would be charmed immediately and want to be around her all the time. But what Daphne knew most of all, was that underneath this attack of pimples, she remembered what she looked like before the breakout: lovely, creamy skin, and once upon a time she had been a really cute girl. In her heart she knew, if only she could get the outside to match.

She loved being home so that she could freely walk around in the clothes she really liked to wear. The clothes she would redesign herself like the white tank top that she tie dyed pink and hot glued swarovski crystals onto the front in the shape of the number 9. She had on low rise corduroy pants and took her shoes off. She wouldn't wear her pants without a sweatshirt to school because it would reveal her little gut and then there would go the "fatty" catcalls. It just never ended, she was absolutely hounded by insults, and only celebrities with the paparazzi following could understand the assault she was under on a daily basis. In the kingdom that was her room, she may not have had any subjects to worship her, but she reigned supreme and she was free to be herself and that was the only thing that mattered to her at the end of the school day. She looked around her room and took pride in the walls that she wallpapered with over 1000 photos of Aquarium. She would cut out every picture she could find from teen magazines and tabloid magazines. She considered floor-to-ceiling photos of the band was almost as good as having the band in her room at all times.

Aquarium was the most popular band in the world. They had held the number 1 spot on the Billboard charts for a record 24 weeks for their single, "Magnolia". The band was currently on tour after the release of their third album. Daphne had all three. She was a huge fan and was hoping they'd come to her town soon so she could see them perform in person. They hadn't booked a date for her town yet, but she held onto hope. Her mom had already agreed to go with her, a rarity for them to go out and do something, but she knew how important the band was to Daphne. The band was always making headlines for who they were dating and what they were wearing. King Crab was the bass guitar player known for his wild hair that he was constantly changing. If it wasn't long and pink, it was short and green and currently he had a blue Mohawk. Shell Salmon was the drummer. In interviews he was the silent one. He wasn't in the original line up, or on the first cd, he joined the band after the original drummer left the band to become a Buddhist monk. Shell recently made the headlines for getting engaged to a supermodel. Fishy Oceans played the rhythm guitar. Daphne didn't know the difference between rhythm and bass guitars; they sounded the same to her: great if it was on her Aquarium cds. Fishy was famous for giving out his guitars at random concerts and for starting a foundation for underprivileged kids to go to music camp and he was also the one member of the band most known for trashing public places. When Daphne watched interviews he talked the most and was funny, she didn't care what she read about his bad behavior, and she felt in her heart he'd get it together.

She glanced at the life size poster of Posiadyn Fisher: lead singer and wicked hot. He stood there, back against a door, his intense, blue eyes gazing back at her and following her every movement around and out of the room. His sexy mouth parted in a way that looked like he was about to say something, and Daphne daydreamed that he was about to reveal all his secrets to her. Secrets like he'd loved her from the moment they met (which of course he would if they ever got the chance), how he wanted her to tour with him, and marry him when she was older, like around 21. Her biggest fantasy was that he would tell her he saw her in a dream long ago, and had been singing to his mysterious, dream girl in all his songs, and she was that beautiful girl. She yearned to be the one he'd been waiting to meet. He was always in the tabloids dating this actress or that dancer. He'd been spotted partying with Gwen Stefani and Christina Aguilera but he hadn't dated anyone for any length of time. Daphne considered her biggest rival to be Britney Spears, she was dead afraid he'd fall for her, but he hadn't. He was saving himself for someone special: her. She was convinced of that.

If only they could meet, then the rest of their lives would begin. Her real life. The life where all her dreams came true and she was beautiful and there weren't two brothers pestering her, a dad who ignored her, or a mother who didn't have time for her.

She moved around on her bed looking for the patent leather purse she kept as her home knitting bag, the remote control digging into her thigh turned her cd player on and Posiadyn's glorious, throaty voice filled the room.

She sang along as she took the knitting needles out of the ball of yarn she was making a baby blanket with.

One of her favorite things to do in the world was to knit. She learned from her grandfather the summer before he passed away. Fondness for that summer caused her heart to swell as she remembered sitting and relaxing with her grandpa as they knitted the hours away. She was there with her brothers that year because it was around the time her parents were splitting up to get divorced. Her mom was having such a hard time dealing with it that her grandpa thought it was best the kids stay with him, while their mom tried to take control of her emotions. The time away that summer didn't do much for her mom's depression and confusion. Daphne felt like a mess most of the time after that, and her brothers, well their spoiled attitudes spoke for themselves. Sitting there with her grandfather those days, she loved listening to his stories of his brothers and sisters, and the history of his European parents. She watched him twiddle his thumbs, sometimes his eye would take on a far away, glassy look and she was his rapt audience. He'd relive his memories of meeting her grandmother, and how he loved her passionately, all those years.

Of all the stories, how he learned to knit was her favorite.

They were going through a hard time after the stillborn birth of their fourth and last child, a little boy they had named Joseph. He would often wake in the middle of the night and find that her grandmother was in the den sitting in his favorite chair knitting the night away. He would try not to disturb her, knowing that she needed the time to herself to heal, so he'd walk through as if to get himself a drink from the kitchen. On one particular night, she sat in the chair, the knitting needles in her lap while she cried. He sat down on the floor beside her feet and took the needles from her lap. He looked at them for a couple minutes because he didn't know what to do. Something inside him told him how to continue on where she left off.

"But I really had no idea what to do with the darned things." He'd told her. In her mind Daphne could hear his voice like she'd just spoken to him, and closed her eyes to let the memory of him live again.

Knit one, purl three, knit one, purl three. He quietly sat there while his wife cried. They didn't speak a word to each other about that night until after a week long of midnight knitting sessions resulted in the creation of a blanket. She had come up to him and said, "We finished the blanket. You know I had intended it to be for the baby, but it's too big now, I guess we'll have to use it." And they used that blanket as a testament of their love, and resolve to get through their tough times together.

Daphne has been knitting ever since. Knowing that you could make something practical, that could serve some purpose to someone made her feel important and like she was making a contribution to someone, anyone. The first throw she knitted took her a few months to finish but she gave it to her mom which they use on the sofa in the living room. It's cozy and they sit under it and watch movies when they're together. She knits scarves and beanies and donates them to the homeless shelters, and she's made two baby blankets that she was very proud to donate to a shelter that houses teenage mothers.

Daphne continued sitting on her bed, knitting while she imagined herself as a famous scarf designer. She couldn't think of anyone famous for designing scarves, but that didn't matter because she would be the one to make scarves hip. She could see herself as an adult, featured in In Style magazine in her studio and her scarves gloriously displayed on mannequins behind her. Every time she went to a Wal-Mart and breezed through their craft department she'd pick up the free page of knitting projects. One day they'd be her knitting projects, if only she knew how to make patterns instead of only following them. But that dream comes second to being on tour with her husband, Posiadyn. When she goes on tour with him, the dream is to take photographs and scrapbook about all the towns they've seen.

Travel and photography seemed real only if she gets to be with Posiadyn. Perhaps it's because she doesn't go anywhere with her mom. And her mom had never mentioned any desire to see any place in the world other than the city where they live. Daphne wants to go everywhere, and see everything. She wants to go to the New York Public library, she wants to go to Tiffany and eat breakfast there. The Golden Gate Bridge, the Washington monument, Las Vegas and Disneyland. When the bands go on tour, they go everywhere! She'd be a picture snapping guru by the time she'd made her way between the pacific and Atlantic coasts.

Her knitting and her daydreams came to a screeching halt when her mom walked into her room. "Hey Daph, you didn't say hi."

"Were you home? Did you park in the garage?"

"Yeah. How was school? Do you want to come down and help me with dinner?" Her mom looked hopefully at her and Daphne couldn't refuse.

Daphne and her mom, Helen, hadn't been close for some time. They both tried, but couldn't seem to quite get it together.

"So, how was school?" Helen asked as she moved around the kitchen.

"Perfectly wretched as usual. They've come up with a new one to call me. Pin cushion face. Can I drop out? Can't you home school me or something? What are we making anyway? I mean mom, nine volt, pizza face, and all the names!" Daphne looked in the fridge to see what was in there.

"I thought we'd make pizzas. You can do the cheese while I work on the dough."

Helen walked to the pantry to gather ingredients. Knowing a battle would begin with what she was about to say, she piled jars of oregano leaves and tomato sauce into her arms while grabbing pepperoni and the mozzarella cheese out of the fridge, and decided to just blurt it out.

"Daphne, I've taken an assignment for the summer, which

means you'll be staying with your dad." Helen was astounded by her own straight forwardness.

"Are you kidding?" Daphne glared at her mother.

"No, I'm not kidding. I've already discussed it with your father. You and the twins will go over there next week."

"Mom, you can't make me go. I won't go." Daphne said defiantly as tears started to spring into her eyes. "And why are you dumping this on me now? How long did you know? Don't I have a say in anything? Whatever, whatever! I'm not going!" Daphne started pacing around the kitchen; she could feel the anger moving her legs, causing her to wring her hands.

"Daph, sweetie, listen to me. I was waiting to tell you until I decided about the job. This is a really great opportunity for me. I'll be doing a semester at sea program which means I'll be teaching on a ship as it cruises around Europe." Helen watched as Daphne paced throughout the kitchen.

"This is a nightmare. Tell me you're joking mom please. Please say it's a joke." Daphne sat down in a chair at the kitchen table; she thought she was going to throw up.

"It's no joke. You'll go next week." Helen sat across from Daphne and tried to hold her hand, but Daphne snatched her hand away.

"You know mom, I have no friends, no one signed my yearbook and I just can't wait to come home where I think I can finally be myself. Now you're telling me I have to spend the summer with the no-show dad and his stupid new wife and that stupid baby and if they think I'm going to baby-sit they better think again!" Daphne couldn't help but raise her voice as the tears streamed down her face. "And, and mom, when did you become so interested in seeing Europe? You haven't taken us anywhere. Ever!"

"Well," Helen paused, her daughter knew how to push her

buttons and make her feel like a terrible mother, "I just didn't always have the money to take us places. And this isn't vacation, it's work. It just happens to be in Europe, which really is a great opportunity for me. Your dad sounded excited that you were coming. And Daphne, I really need a break."

"Why wouldn't he be excited? If he thinks I'm going to babysit he better think again! Please mom, don't make me go!"

Helen had reached her own limit and she stood up, "How selfish are you! Don't you think I deserve a little time to myself?"

Daphne stood up too, "No I don't! You are the mom aren't you! He started a new family remember!"

"How can I forget? Do you think I'm putting on all this weight because I like it?"

"I don't have time to think about your weight problem mom, I'm too busy stressing out about my own."

Mother and daughter stood defiantly against one another, eye to eye like a matador and his bull.

Ryan and Ritchie walked in allowing Helen the distraction from her daughter's pained eyes to turn her attention to the boys.

"Well boys, you're going to spend the summer with your dad. You'll go there next week."

The boys shrieked with joy as they jumped up and down for a couple moments then ran out of the kitchen as fast as they had run in.

Helen looked hopefully at Daphne who ran out of the room crying. Helen watched her go as energy seeped out of her body and anxiety creeped in. She did the best she could with her kids, not that they could understand. She knew she made a huge mistake by falling apart after the divorce, she had tried to keep it together, but the stress beat her. The shock of hearing him say he was leaving could still bring shivers to her arms. She looked at the pizza ingredients on the kitchen counters and left them there, instead making some sandwiches and leaving them on the counter with some chips for the kids to eat when they wanted. She would take a bath and simply try again tomorrow.

While Helen slipped out of her clothes and into a warm bath, Daphne had her head buried in a pillow and sobbed. She flailed on her bed kicking it and beat down the sides with clenched fists. When she finally came up for air, she looked for her Posiadyn Fisher bobblehead, her latest crafty novelty. She taped a picture of him onto one of her little brother's bobbleheads and that was it, but now it escaped her in the sea of scrap booking supplies that covered her bedside table.

"Can you believe it Posiadyn? She called me selfish, I mean she actually called me selfish and she's the one leaving! And she expects me to be happy because the twins are. Whatever!" the anger welled up in her causing her to growl her words. If she could scream at the top of her lungs she would but she knew she couldn't. She didn't have screaming lungs.

An idea came to her and she jumped off her bed with a bolt. Rushing around her room she sought out her favorite things to put in a duffle bag: knitting needles, yarn, her Aquarium scrapbook, a few clothes and a couple more crafting supplies.

"I'll show her!" she huffed and puffed as she went to her window to open it. There was no way she was going to spend the summer with that man and she was going to show her mom that she couldn't make her.

Looking at the two stories down below her window, Daphne realized there was no way out but to jump. She didn't have jumping legs, and dejectedly she threw the duffle bag on her bed.

"Who am I kidding" she hollered and then turned up the volume on her stereo. She turned it up as high as she could knowing it would totally aggravate her mother. Then she buried her head into the pillow, giving up to her fate.

2

The week before Daphne left for what she considered her summer imprisonment, she had a blast ignoring her mother and staying in her room. It was what she thought of as "Daphne's Retreat". She relaxed because she had no idea what it would be like to have to live with a baby. She had no idea how old her baby sister was, but she didn't care. She didn't plan on hanging out with the little brat at all. Daphne enjoyed the week by making scrapbook pages of Posiadyn, and started a new scarf that she wanted to mail to him for his birthday. She found what she considered an amazing shade of sky blue yarn that matched the color of his eyes. He was such a dreamboat and as she knitted her last few nights away before imprisonment, she wondered if he'd ever actually wear it. She couldn't see why not, the blue wasn't girlie at all. Didn't guys wear scarves too?

The days melted one into the next and she wasn't even aware they were passing by. No matter how hard she tried to hide in her room, and deny that she'd actually have to spend the whole summer with the enemies, the day had come for her dad to pick her up. Of course it was the hottest day of summer. A sweat inducing, miserable day of eighty something degrees and no matter how much water or lemonade she drank she couldn't keep her dry mouth quenched. She was convinced it was probably some kind of foreshadowing of the hellish summer she was in store for.

While she waited for her dad to come, she couldn't knit, she couldn't think, all she could do was sit on the couch and tap her feet. She looked around the living room and noted that her mom had straightened up. No video game cords strung out anywhere, all the boys' toys put away nicely in their room. The bookshelves were lined neatly, not a spec of dust or spider's web to be seen anywhere. Daphne could feel bitterness begin to flood her thoughts as the considered that her mom was going away on some fabulous vacation while she was being sent away to a firing squad. Her mom had even dressed up and put on makeup this morning although dressed up was that instead of wearing her usual sweat pants and sweatshirt she'd thrown on a pair of jeans and a button down blouse in a fabric she didn't recognize. Maybe it was rayon? Daphne was thinking of every fabric she could remember as she eyed her mom as she walked frantically in and out of the living room and made sure to note her rump was looking larger than usual. The jeans weren't flattering at all. As if her dad would even notice, Daphne knew it was all a show for him.

"Packing some junk in the trunk mom, you're better off putting your sweats back on." She quipped and when her mom stopped in front of her with a dirty look Daphne knew the remark hurt her feelings and she didn't even care. She'd say it one hundred more times if it'd keep her from having to go to her dad's.

The moment she saw his Escalade pull into the driveway she felt her stomach do a flip flop and thought she would throw up. She put a hand to her mouth because suddenly her legs felt like bricks and all she could do is continue to sit there feeling like a lump of crap. An absolute lump of nothing worth anything since her mom was shipping off and shipping Daphne out to the enemy. Ryan and Ritchie were running around the house like banshees screaming about the arrival. They were acting like their hero had just showed up. Kids! She thought as she made a huff and folded her arms in front of her chest. Daphne considered no man she hadn't seen in years a hero. She was trying to think of how long it actually had been and remembered that the last time she saw him, he'd invited them to meet their new baby sister in the hospital which seemed like ten years ago. And of course they didn't go, their mom wouldn't let them and they had to listen to her crying in her room all night. It was going to be horrible; she was positively convinced she'd probably die the first week she was there.

He walked in, each twin holding one of his hands. He was tall and wore dark blue jeans and some button down shirt in a material that looked soft and expensive the color of butter yellow. What kind of man wore butter yellow? He was whipped for sure and Holly, the brutal wife probably picked it out. Butter yellow, butter yellow, it kept going off in her mind like popcorn kernels that wouldn't stop popping. Butter yellow. Posiadyn Fisher wouldn't be caught dead in a butter yellow shirt, he was way to hip and cool for that. She tried not to look at him, but she was curious. He had a smile on his face, she would never admit it, but it was a warm smile and he looked happy to see her, but she wouldn't be that easily won over. As he stood before her she tried not to let him intimidate her, so in an effort to show him who was boss she briefly glanced towards his direction and rolled her eyes.

"Hey you! Are you ready to go?" he asked. She thought he had some nerve to act so happy to see her when she couldn't remember the last time she saw him. He came over and stood directly in front of her she knew he was waiting for her to stand up and give him a hug but she was doing everything she could think of to show him that she thought he was a jerk, and certainly didn't deserve any affection from her.

"Mom is in the kitchen, she wanted to talk to you before we left." Daphne said, still avoiding eye contact and keeping her arms folded in front of her chest.

"No problem." He handed her the keys, "want to start putting your stuff in the car?"

Daphne looked at him incredulously wondering why she had to do it, but she took the keys and headed out the door. "It figures, the nightmare begins." She muttered to herself. Already he's telling her what to do and making her do everything. She was furious as she picked up her bags and yelled at her brothers to get going.

In the kitchen, Helen tried to busy herself by loading the dishwasher. Seeing her ex-husband always caused her tremendous amounts of anxiety. She was still bitter and wondered if she'd ever forgive him, or ever forget the problems they had.

"Helen, Daphne said you wanted to talk." He said.

She looked at her husband, still handsome as ever. His long frame leaned easily against the counter, his dark hair still not showing any gray although he was in his mid 40's. Unconsciously she started slamming the dishes into the slots, angrily thinking how unfair it was that she's put on 40 pounds and regularly has to get her hair colored.

"Well Daphne is angry at having to spend the summer with you and I don't know how cooperative she'll be. She holed herself up in her room and has barely spoken to any of us for the last week."

"She'll be fine. Holly spent a lot of time decorating her room, trying to make it nice for her and has a lot planned this summer."

Helen turned away from him at the mention of *her* name.

Sensing the tension, Todd touched her shoulder.

"Can't we get through this? It could be so much better on all of us if you could just try."

"Try? Try what? What kind of role model is that woman to my children? A home wrecking slut..." Todd cut her off before she could finish.

"Enough, stop right there." Todd was firm, but Helen continued.

"That woman who couldn't find herself her own husband!" she was screaming as she turned and noticed Daphne standing in the entry.

"Can't you guys stop fighting? I thought that's why you got divorced!" Daphne ran outside.

"You know Helen, you were very unhappy too. Blaming Holly forever will get you nowhere." Todd said goodbye and followed Daphne out to the car.

As they drove the short distance between the two homes, the boys rattled on about how much fun they were planning to have over the summer.

"Holly and I are really happy you kids are staying with us this summer." He said hopefully as he drove down the street.

"I'm sure you are. I don't do baby sitting, just so you know." She looked out the window at the houses as they whizzed by. Her father lived in a community near to where Daphne lived but the houses were only a few years old. It aggravated her more remembering that they did live pretty close yet she never saw him. She noticed that the houses were much bigger, and all the lawns had fresh, very green grass. The grass in her yard was spotted with green and brown spots in the front yard and back. She wondered that her dad could probably afford people to come mow their grass, and water it too. She couldn't get her mom to pay her to do it so Daphne refused. The boys were too young, and her mom was lazy or depressed or whatever her problem was, so they had spotted grass and were going to a place where the grass was taken care of and beautiful. Daphne continued to seethe internally.

Daphne could see Holly playing in the front yard of the house as soon as they turned onto the street. Her blonde hair, a few shades lighter than her mom's was flowing in the gentle breeze. She was sitting on the grass, watching Daphne's baby half-sister run around the yard. It was as if the moment was happening in slow motion as she watched Holly laughing and as they approached the front of the house Daphne saw her jump up and wave to them enthusiastically. Her huge, happy smile was hard to miss. Daphne wanted to throw up.

"The baby is getting so big!" Ritchie said.

"Look at the puppies!" Ryan said.

Daphne watched as her sister ran excitedly after the puppies that ran up to the car.

"Hi boys!" Holly said as they jumped out and she gave them big bear hugs.

"Look at the puppies!" Ryan said again as he started to chase the dogs. The puppies were actually a pair of wiener dogs, one was all black, the other was cream colored and although Daphne thought they were the cutest things she ever saw, running on the grass like they were chasing a race horse, she wouldn't crack a smile to save her life.

Todd climbed out and Daphne waited a moment before she got out too. She watched her dad kiss Holly on the forehead, a simple gesture that broke Daphne's heart. Holly was so young and pretty and sparkly compared to her mom who looked old and weathered. Holly looked easily put together and fashionable; her mom always looked like she had to try to look even remotely decent. Daphne suddenly felt sad for her mom and couldn't find her footing for all the different emotions she was experiencing and in a split second she went tumbling out of the car.

"God dammit!" Daphne screamed and as she heard it come out of her mouth she didn't mean to say it, but she was so confused and forgot for a second how high the car was. She fell on her side, thank god for the extra pounds because it didn't hurt. Her pride was hurt more. She didn't want Princess Holly to see her looking any more awkward than she was already beginning to feel. Todd and Holly came over asking if she was okay but she shooed them away as she tried to get up. She was embarrassed and just wanted to hide. She was fighting back tears although they had already started to fill up her eyes. She pretended not to notice that they were just standing there looking at her and each other before Holly finally spoke.

"Daphne, I'm so excited that you're here." Daphne noticed that it looked like Holly wanted to give her a hug, but wasn't sure if she should.

"Whatever." And Daphne went into the backseat to retrieve her bags.

"I spent a lot of time working on your room. Trying to make it special for you."

"That's good. I plan on spending all summer there." Daphne tried to muster all the sarcasm in her veins as she took her stuff and headed towards the house. Daphne could imagine how "special" it would be. It was probably girlie and pink with frilly cotton comforters and eyelet curtains. How else could someone decorate a room for someone they barely knew? Daphne promised herself to hate it.

Daphne stood in the living room looking around. She hadn't been to their new home yet and was angry as she looked at all the comfortable furniture. She glanced at the overstuffed sofa and matching loveseat and a huge cozy looking chair that Daphne was dying to sit in. Tons of pillows were everywhere and a few stuffed animals on the floor. They had a big screen television with the video games set up and ready for the boys to play. She noted a furry rug on the floor that looked like some animals had to die to make it and she made a mental note to hate Holly even more for being cruel to animals. She'd make sure to mention something about PETA the first chance she got. She couldn't find her words at that moment though because there was so much warmth and love flowing in the room that Daphne tried to fight the fact that she could actually feel the love and warmth. It was clean and clutter free, unlike her home, and resentment started to boil up inside her. She hated the fact that her dad had a new life, a new baby, a pretty young wife. His life seemed so much better than hers and she hated him for it. She hated him for not being a part of her life, hated the cute baby sister who toddled around and was standing next to her waiting to be acknowledged. Hated the fact that even their dogs were cute and perfect and all of it made Daphne feel that much more fat, pimply, and completely out of place.

Holly picked up on Daphne's anger because as soon as she entered she immediately took her bags and wouldn't look at her.

"Well, follow me."

They walked down the hall in silence.

"You go first." Holly said as she stood in front of a door with a little plaque with pink and blue mosaic tiles that spelled out her name.

Daphne opened the door and gasped as she stepped in and all her anger and resentment turned into a puddle of shame at her feet as she took in the sight before her eyes. On the wall facing her was a mural of her favorite band, Aquarium. They stood lined up next to each other, Posiadyn Fisher in the center and towards the front. She'd never seen anything like it and squealed in delight as she walked over to the wall and touched the bigger than life image of her dream man. They looked so real, as if they were actually standing in the room with her and Daphne couldn't take her eyes off it.

"How did you know?" was all she could mutter.

"Who doesn't love Aquarium?" Holly grinned as she held the baby and Todd stood behind her. The boys ran in.

"Wow!" They exclaimed as the three of them stood before the mural.

"She thinks she's going to marry him." Ryan said.

"Who would marry her?" Ritchie said. Daphne was in such shock and sheer pleasure that she ignored the remark which ordinarily would have upset her.

"How did you do this?" Daphne asked, still unable to look anywhere but at the mural as she sat down in front of it, unable to look at anything else.

"I have a friend who's a painter…he owed me a favor." Holly said.

"Did you do something for our room?" Ritchie asked.

"Yeah, I had some fun with it, let's go." Todd said as he and the boys turned around.

"I don't know what to say. Thank you." Daphne grinned but still couldn't look at Holly. "I didn't think it'd be possible I'd want to stay here forever, but now I don't know how I could find the will to leave." Daphne gushed and the dogs jumped in her lap sniffing her arms and trying to lick her face.

"Well, I have a lot planned for you. This is only the beginning." Holly smiled as she started to walk out.

"My best friend lives next door and we're planning a barbecue for you all. I'll come get you after awhile." Holly stood there for a moment, and then said, "I'm really looking forward to having you here Daphne. I think it's going to be a great time." Daphne finally looked at Holly, and wanted to believe her.

Daphne sat in front of the mural for a long time. She hadn't even looked around to notice anything else in the room although she knew it was cute and it wasn't pink and frilly. She just looked at Posiadyn, standing so lifelike right in front of her and promised that she'd talk to him all summer long.

Only when Holly came up to get her for the barbecue did she finally move.

"I think it's kind of nice your friend wants to have a barbecue for us." Daphne said, following Holly out to the kitchen.

"Yeah, we like to get together as often as possible." Holly smiled as she worked around the kitchen, "why don't you get the covered dishes out of the fridge for me."

As Daphne maneuvered around the kitchen with all its shiny and new appliances she couldn't help the pangs of jealousy begin to creep into her system again. Everything about her dad's life seemed so much better than her own. Friends coming over and caring enough about each other to barbecue. She couldn't remember the last time she had a friend, someone to share secrets with and talk about Posiadyn Fisher. Her mom never barbecued and she had no idea who any of her neighbors were.

"So are you excited about starting high school?" Holly said with a smile on her face. Daphne wondered if Holly ever had a bad day, she seemed like she was constantly happy, with a smile plastered across her face at all times. She thought to herself it would probably become very annoying living with someone like that the entire summer. She was used to scowls, frowns and insults from her little brothers.

"Not quite. I'm hoping I can be home schooled or something.

Maybe get a tutor. Anything to not go back. Maybe I'll even drop out."

"That sounds a little melodramatic." Holly said.

"Well you don't know my life."

Holly stopped puttering around the kitchen and stood next to Daphne. She touched her arm and said, "I'd like to know your life. I'd really like to be your friend."

Daphne could hear Helen's voice echoing in her brain about Holly the home wrecker, Holly the slut. Daphne truly hated the word slut. She remembered the bitter argument she got into with her mom the first time she'd heard her mom say it. She felt torn between needing to hate Holly, and maybe wanting to give her a chance at the same time. Anyone who gave her a huge mural of Aquarium was A-OK in Daphne's book.

"They just call me names all the time." Daphne's eyes started to tear and she turned away, "names I can hardly repeat, god, you'd think no one saw braces before, and now I've put on this weight. It's always something with the kids at school, I can't get over it."

"Are you feeling a little depressed and overeating?"

Daphne looked out the window into their backyard. Daphne didn't really want to talk about her problems with Miss Perfect Holly. She looked out the window at Holly's friends milling around, her dad at the grill, her siblings playing. Then Daphne caught a glimpse of the last person in the world she'd ever expect in her own dad's backyard.

"That isn't Nicole Gaines is it?"

"Yeah," Holly brightened, "do you know her?"

"Holly, I'm sorry, but I can't go out there." Daphne ducked from the window, hoping that Nicole hadn't caught a glimpse of her already.

Nicole Gaines was the most popular girl in school.

Stereotypical petite blonde, she was gorgeous with flawless skin and beautiful teeth. No acne or braces for her, she seemed to be naturally pretty. Always dressed in the trendiest outfits she had style that Daphne envied, she was able to put outfits together in a way that no other girls at school could and she never looked like she walked out of the pages of a magazine or like she shopped at the mall although it was obvious she did. She had true style and flair that was original and Daphne only had it in secrecy in her room at home. But for everything outwardly enviable, she was equally nasty. She would often call Daphne dirty names as they passed in the hallway. When Daphne walked into the math class they shared, after her face had broken out for the first time, Nicole at the top of her voice asked Daphne if she had the chicken pox. The class then went into a round of clucking noises. Needless to say, Daphne ran out in tears to the nurse's office and went home for the day. None of which she would dare mention to Holly.

"Oh, that's right, you guys go to the same school don't you? She is one of sweetest girls I've ever met." Holly smiled sweetly and Daphne wanted to hit her.

"Sweet? Are you kidding? Whatever, you don't go to school with her." Daphne couldn't help but steal peeks out the window to make sure Nicole hadn't seen her, or worse than that, try to come in.

"I can guarantee you that she won't cause any trouble in front of her mom. Around here, she is really a kind, generous girl."

Daphne wouldn't argue.

Daphne followed Holly outside and when Nicole saw Daphne her face lost all color and she shot Daphne a dirty look. Holly didn't miss a beat and was bewildered to see this side of the young girl she thought she knew.

"Nicole, I never put it together that you may know my step

daughter Daphne. She told me how much fun you two have at school." Daphne didn't miss the irony that Holly was getting at. She was very smooth and earned points on her coolness meter.

Nicole smiled, not knowing how to respond, but catching on that Holly knew she was not friendly to Daphne.

"Yeah, unfortunately, we don't get to hang out that much."

"She'll be here all summer, that should give you plenty of time to catch up." Holly sat down next to Nicole's mom, Tammy, and watched Nicole shrink into her chair.

"I forgot something in the house, I'll be back." Daphne excused herself relieved to get out of the presence of someone she considered an enemy. She couldn't believe how the number on the enemy side kept going up, at that rate she'd probably find out Ty Stone lived across the street and they all take vacations together. The idea was too much to bare. In her new haven, Daphne sat on the floor in front of her mural and worked on Posiadyn's scarf as she talked to him as he loomed larger than life on her wall.

"And then, Nicole Gaines of all people, mortal enemy, nemesis, whatever...she lives next door." She put down her knitting to contemplate, and then picked it up again, "I mean what can I do? I don't think I have the energy to contend with Holly and Nicole. Although Holly might not be so bad after all, I'll have to wait and see about her. But I mean Nicole Gaines, she's so thin, and so pretty and I..." Daphne suddenly had an idea. She put her knitting down again and lay on her back. She was resolved to start a diet and exercise regime. She tried to do a sit up, but could barely get her back up off the floor. She rolled over and tried to do a push up, but she couldn't go down. Huffing and puffing she called it quits.

"Can't even do a single push up or sit up. Posiadyn, what am I going to do?" She looked at his handsome face. "I'll worry about it in the morning."

Daphne looked out the window at the festivities outside. It was late and they were all still out there. She couldn't spy Nicole anywhere thank god. Daphne imagined she was out with all the other popular kids talking about her and how fat she was

She'd had a long day and just wanted to get some sleep. It was all so emotional, and so confusing.

That first night Daphne was easily able to drift off to sleep which she hadn't expected. Maybe it was the silent peace that filled the air of her dad's home. Maybe it was because the love of her life stood over her and watched her sleep. Something in Daphne felt changed somehow. She felt comfortable, and despite the fact that her dad and home had not been synonymous for a very long time, she felt like she was home and she felt protected for the first time in a very long time. She was used to staying up most the night for fear she'd miss something. What she thought she'd miss she had no idea, but she always put off falling to sleep. It's just what she did. Sleeping easily was a welcome change to her routine.

Daphne was settling in decently enough. She spent a lot of time in her room, sitting on the floor knitting and talking to Posiadyn as he stood on her wall. She appreciated that no one really bothered her and let her listen to her music as loud as she wanted. She was saving money that her dad kept giving her to "enjoy herself". She had quite a savings started up and decided one afternoon that she might "enjoy herself" by tagging along with Holly and the kids to Wal-Mart.

Shopping with all the kids was a complete joke. The twins ran up and down all the aisles while the baby grabbed for everything and threw it in the basket. Holly kept her composure through the whole event and Daphne had no idea where her patience came from. She was getting so irritated she took off by herself to find a jump rope.

She looked through the beauty aisles. She knew herself around a Sephora like a racehorse knows its way around a race track, cosmetics were her thing. But hair products and waxing products was something else entirely different. She desperately wanted to work on herself over the summer. If she was going to be forced to go to school, she was going to do what she could to fit in this year. Her first idea was to try to shape her own eyebrows and buy a frosting kit. She read the directions on the backs of the boxes and it was like trying to read German, she was positive she'd probably mess something up.

As she walked up to the registers to find Holly, a tabloid headline caught her eye.

"Posiadyn engaged!" The headline caught her attention like a neon sign and Daphne's heart sank as she picked up the magazine which had a picture of her beloved Posiadyn sitting with his arm around a pretty redhead. She felt herself begin to hyperventilate as she read the article and walked up to Holly standing in line.

"Don't believe everything you read! Poor guy gets no privacy." Holly said as she piled her things on the conveyor belt.

"I wonder who the girl is. Oh my god, Holly, who do you think she is, I think I'm going to die, my chest hurts. Am I having a heart attack?" she took the magazine and fanned herself for a second before the curiosity got the best of her again and she continued reading the article.

"Probably some dancer on tour with him that they got a photo of and are now making it into something else. Did you hear about when he was having an affair with his stylist?" Holly asked.

"I was devastated!" Daphne laughed; surprised that Holly even knew who he was.

"Remember the one that said his mom was suing him because he hadn't called her in months?"

"I know. I thought, here we go Eminem. Do you think Posiadyn Fisher is hot?" she leaned closer to Holly as if she were about to give her the most important information of her life.

"He's pretty cute." Holly smiled. "I have a feeling he's probably really nice."

Daphne was beginning to like Holly more and more.

After paying for her new found beauty and exercise supplies, getting all the kids in the car and listening to various twin chatter, baby babbling and screaming, Daphne swore she'd never go shopping again. The whole loud scene they all made embarrassed her and she couldn't wait to get to her room and start reading instructions on brow shaping.

As the music of Aquarium blared through the hallway, Daphne stood in the bathroom. The bottles and needles of a frosting kit littered the counter as the frosting cap covered her head. She sang along with the lyrics as she stirred a tub of thick wax wondering how she'd be able to tell if it was ready. She impatiently applied it to her brows and upper lip. She pulled the wax off her lip and cringed only a little, noting it hadn't hurt as bad as she expected it to. When she ripped the wax off her brow, it did cause tears to spring to her eyes, but just barely. She looked at herself in the mirror to admire her handiwork, considering for a moment that maybe she should be a cosmetologist.

Daphne looked at herself in the mirror and thought something just didn't look right. As she examined her face closer in the mirror, she let out a scream.

The twins rushed into the bathroom.

"What are you doing?" Ritchie asked.

"Can we watch you, we're bored." Ryan said.

"Why do you look funny?" Ritchie asked.

Daphne ran into the living room where Holly was clearing some toys off the floor.

"Oh my god, oh my god. Holly look what I did!" Daphne felt herself begin to hyperventilate, "Oh my god, I think I'm having a heart attack."

"What happened?" Holly asked looking at her face and the strands of her dark hair hanging out of the holes in the frosting cap.

"You can't see that, you can't see what I did?" Daphne asked frantically pointing to face.

"What?" Holly asked looking her up and down.

"I waxed off my eyebrow!"

Holly looked at Daphne's face and burst into laughter.

"How did you do that?" Holly asked.

"I don't know."

"Don't worry Daphne, two words, eyebrow pencil. It will be fine."

"Oh my god! My hair!"

Daphne ran back into the bathroom to rinse her hair out in the sink tears beginning to spill out of her eyes. She grabbed a towel and tried to towel dry it before she looked at herself in the mirror.

Daphne screamed again and this time Holly ran in with the twins.

"Oh my god! Fire ball!" Ryan said laughing.

"I just want to look like everyone else. I just want to be normal." Daphne said as she sat on the toilet and covered her face with her hands.

"What color were you going for?" Holly asked as she took strands of Daphne's hair in her hands to examine.

"I was just trying to frost it." Daphne couldn't control herself now, she couldn't stop crying. It was all too much. Instead of evenly frosted streaks of hair, she had chunks of red and blonde and her natural dark brown.

"I guess you didn't time it right?" Holly offered hopefully.

"I don't know." Daphne said.

Daphne felt defeated. She had to do something different if she'd be living next door to Nicole Gaines all summer. Daphne was afraid if something drastic didn't happen to her appearance, it would be a matter of time before Nicole started yelling out names to her from the front yard. So far none of Daphne's attempts to look like other teenagers were working. She sat sobbing on the toilet, her face buried in her hands.

Holly sat on the floor mat at Daphne's feet.

"Listen, I'll make an appointment for you with my hairdresser ok? It'll be fine, and you'll look great. Daphne, let's make an agreement ok?"

Daphne looked into Holly's kind blue eyes, feeling drained she waited to hear what she had to say.

"If you need or want anything, just let me know. I'm sorry I wasn't paying attention to what you were buying or I would have offered already. Sometimes I get a little overwhelmed, but it doesn't mean that I don't care about you. I mean it, anything you want or need, just let me know."

Daphne hugged her before she knew what she was doing. She was already feeling very conflicted about this home wrecking woman who sat at her feet. She was beautiful, fun and happy. She acted like she cared, and even wanted to get to know her and maybe become friends. But she was also the woman who came in between her mother and father. This was the woman who turned her mom into a crying, selfish, unstable mess. This woman took her father away.

Daphne stiffened, said thank you and walked back to her room.

It was only a couple days that Daphne had to walk around with half an eyebrow and flames of color streaking her hair. Tres Belle, the salon that Holly frequented was an exclusive one according to her mother. In an affluent neighborhood, it was a very old remodeled house that they turned into a salon and every time they drove by her mom would wistfully remind her how exclusive it was and how she wished she could afford to go there, just once. Her mother had explained that she heard that when you entered the salon they immediately served you champagne, and that when movies were filmed in town the stylists and makeup artists from that salon only were called to the set. Daphne had noticed that when she watched the nightly news it would say, "Styling and makeup courtesy of Tres Belle". Daphne felt guilty that she was going there now. She felt like she shouldn't be at this place without her mom. Holly started to get out of the car and Daphne stayed seated.

"What's wrong?" Holly asked, bending down into the car.

"Isn't it expensive here?" Daphne looked towards the salon wondering what it was like inside.

"Daph, don't worry about those things. It's not a problem." Holly walked to Daphne's side of the car and opened the door. They walked through the parking lot and Daphne wouldn't look around for fear that someone would see her multi colored hair. She noticed that all the cars were expensive types like BMWs and she couldn't escape the guilt of being there with Holly and not her mom.

Once inside, Daphne noted that all the girls looked like they walked off a Cover Girl commercial. Every one of them had legs the size of Daphne's arms, looked like they were in high school and was breathtakingly beautiful. They were the type of women that she always secretly hoped she would become. They all looked glamorous, they looked like not only should they be on the arm of Posiadyn Fisher, but they belonged there, as if they were born solely to walk along red carpets at the Grammy's in designer dresses.

"Holly! Where is that gorgeous baby of yours?" Said a girl, with the prettiest, long brown hair Daphne had ever seen. Shiny with no visible split ends it looked thick and certainly had no orange streaks going through it, she couldn't believe that even someone's hair could actually be so perfect. She had huge blue eyes too, like fish eyes sparkling at her. She wore a flowy top that Daphne recognized as chiffon with skinny jeans and pointy toed heels that clacked on the floor when she walked. Daphne wondered if the girl was real, and glanced around looking for some sort of virtual reality device.

"Tammy has her. This is Daphne, my step daughter." Holly said and smiled as she took Daphne's hand.

The beautiful girl smiled at Daphne and introduced herself as Bree.

"I went to beauty school so that I'd quit giving myself flames," she whispered into Daphne's ear as she led her to a stool.

"Candace will be here in a moment." Bree said and walked away.

"She's not doing my hair?" Daphne asked, convinced that someone with such beautiful hair could transform her mop into hair that would be on the boxes of hair color everywhere.

"No, but here comes Candace now." Holly smiled and walked over to stunning redhead with a smile so wide that Daphne could count her teeth.

"Hi Daphne, I've heard so much about you! What are we going to do today?" Candace had a sing song way of speaking.

Daphne was speechless, and incredulous that so many beautiful people could be found in one place.

"You have beautiful eyes Daphne. If you're allowed to wear makeup we have a make up artist that can work with you if you'd like?" she talked to Daphne through the mirror while she combed her hands through Daphne's hair.

Daphne looked between Candace and Holly.

"Just let me know." Holly said.

"But I don't have any makeup." Daphne looked at herself in the mirror.

"Don't worry cupcake, we have everything you need here." Candace said as she put the cape around Daphne.

Daphne closed her eyes, hoping that when she opened them, she would fit in at this place of pristine, flawless beauty. She knew she had a lot of work to do to become as beautiful as they were, but in this place anything seemed possible. Getting her hair washed and her head massaged was a dream. She wondered why her head didn't tingle that way when she washed her own hair. Her hair was dried, sprayed wet, cut, put under a dryer, colored and when she finally saw her image in the mirror, she couldn't keep the tears from pouring down her face. Whereas when Daphne walked in she had multi-colored, frizzy, fly away hair, now her hair was one shade of dark brown with reddish blonde highlights and straightened, looking longer although it had just been cut and styled differently than anything she'd ever been able to do. She now understood what "exclusive" means: that you become exclusive too.

"Sweetie, you're so sensitive. You look beautiful." Holly said.

"Thank you." Was all Daphne could say.

Bree and Candace and a couple other stylists had come over to look at her new hairstyle. Even her eyebrows looked normal.

"This was a dream come true. I love it." Daphne hugged Holly and for the first time since summer began she really wanted to hold her. For the first time in her life, Daphne wanted to go somewhere, to show off and to be seen. She wasn't used to that feeling.

"Is there somewhere we can go?" Daphne asked.

"Sure, we can go the mall and have some lunch?"

Daphne could hardly contain her excitement and heard

herself talk non stop. She talked about her knitting, about Posiadyn Fisher, her favorite songs, how maybe now, she wanted to be a hair stylist.

They walked around the mall after having some pizza and stopping at Sephora for her favorite lip-gloss. Daphne had not known herself to be such a chatter box because she didn't stop talking until she saw Nicole walking around with Ty Stone, and another popular girl from school, Celia Johnson.

"Holly I've been trying so hard to keep my mouth shut about Nicole, but see her over there and that girl she's with?"

Holly looked in the direction Daphne was looking and saw Nicole who smiled and waved in their direction

"That girl, Celia, her and Nicole have the worst reputation and I heard a rumor that they got into a fight with this thirty year-old woman and that Celia almost kicked her ass." Daphne looked sheepishly at Holly, "sorry..."

"You said ass. So what. What is this about a fight? With a woman? And Nicole was there?" Holly's motherly instinct kicked into gear.

"I don't know, it was just all over school." Daphne sipped on her drink, feeling fabulous and not really caring anything about Nicole.

When they finally got home, her dad couldn't compliment her enough on how great her hair looked. She could feel herself blush and was thrilled at all the attention he was paying to her. She felt so good inside she even took her baby sister Georgie, up to her room with her. Daphne danced around the room and laughed as the baby would sway back and forth trying to dance. Or bend her knees and move up and down as she drank from her bottle. Daphne was so happy at the bonds she was making. She couldn't think of a time in her life when she felt so free. She was comfortable, and anything seemed possible.

As she watched her little sister dance and wave her arms she had memories of her mom coming home from work and just sitting on their couch in silence. Daphne couldn't remember how young she was, but she'd go up to her mom who would stare off into space as her twin brothers cried. Daphne remembered wondering where her dad was and as she pondered, what drove a man to leave his family, she couldn't help but wonder if it was her mom's fault. What started it? Daphne had a feeling that her parents had both been very unhappy. How could she recognize peace, when tension hung so thick in the air of her home for as long as she could remember? How do you know if you're happy or unhappy if you have nothing to compare it to? In this new home, her dad pays attention to her, and everyone talks to each other, and hangs out together. How bad could that really be? Daphne wondered if she had the courage to talk to her dad about it. Could she bring it up to Holly? She knew asking her mom was out of the question.

Daphne felt the sudden urge to hug Georgie. She realized how lucky her little sister was to have a happy mom and dad who loved her to raise her, and how happy she was for her. Maybe her mom and dad just weren't meant to be. It was a thought she wanted to get to the bottom of.

Finding the time to get her dad alone for a chat wasn't easy because they were constantly doing things together or having barbecues. Barbecues were a common gathering at Daphne's dad's house. She'd only actually run into Nicole at the first one. Nicole was usually gone with her friends and Daphne was beginning to think that she might not have to hide out in order to avoid Nicole.

Daphne was sitting on a lounge chair watching Georgie play with the dogs when Nicole approached her.

"Hi! Can I sit with you?" Before Daphne could respond, Nicole was sitting on the grass next to her chair.

"You can get a chair." Daphne said as she started to get up. "No, I'm fine here. I like the feel of the cool grass against my skin." Daphne tried to avoid eye contact, not sure of what Nicole would want if she wanted to sit with her.

"I like your new hair. It looks great, it suits you." Nicole said as she smiled.

"Thanks." A compliment from Nicole Gaines? Daphne tried not to act like she'd just won the lottery, but she was so excited that this popular girl who used to ridicule her had actually just paid her a sincere compliment. She didn't really know how to respond. She was terrified that Nicole would humiliate her somehow and was waiting for her to turn on her.

"Hey can you show me your room? I've been dying to see it, I heard all about it while Holly was doing it." Nicole started to get up.

"You want to see my room?" Daphne was aghast trying to think if there was a mess anywhere that might embarrass her. "Ok, let me get the baby."

Georgie didn't want to go inside the house so Daphne led Nicole into the room.

Daphne could see Nicole's excitement as soon as she walked in. Her face broke into the biggest smile she'd ever noticed, she turned in every direction trying to take it all in.

"OH MY GOSH!! It looks even better than I thought. She worked so hard on everything in here for you. She made that quilt for you." Nicole pointed to the quilt that covered her bed.

"Really? She made it? How do you know?" Daphne asked.

"I'd come over and sit with her sometimes, and she'd be cutting out fabric, sewing, whatever. She's been working on it for years. I haven't seen it until now." Nicole said as she walked to the bed and sat on it.

Daphne was silently impressed. Nicole said she'd worked on it for years? What did that mean? Had Holly been thinking about Daphne all this time?

"Posiadyn Fisher is such a dream! I think the drummer Fishy is hotter though." Nicole giggled as she flipped on the stereo.

"Shut up!" Daphne said as she sat on the floor in front of it.

Nicole sat next to her, "is this what you do? Sit on the floor and stare at him all day?"

"Pretty much." Daphne giggled.

"I would too." Nicole stared at awe alongside her.

They were silent for a moment and the awkwardness caused Daphne to spring to her feet.

"Do you have any hobbies? I like to knit." She grabbed her knitting bag and pulled out some yarn from the latest scarf she was making.

"Not really. I like to write poetry, but that's not a hobby is it?"

"I don't see why not. I also scrapbook, do you want to see my Aquarium scrapbook?" Daphne said as she pulled it out from under her bed.

"Why is it under there?" Nicole asked as she started to flip through the pages.

"I don't know, I'm afraid it'll get stolen. I have thousands of pictures in there. In my room back home, I have 65 posters of them hanging on my wall." Daphne bragged, "well, along with hundreds of pictures I've taped to my wall."

"That's a lot of Popstar." Nicole said and they both laughed.

There was awkward silence again and finally Daphne said, "Are you trying to be nice to me?"

"Yeah, I think I'd really like to be your friend."

"Why?" Daphne asked, afraid to hear the answer.

"Besides the fact that my mom told me she'd kill me if I didn't make friends with you?"

Daphne cringed and felt the tears burn her eyes. Seeing how hurt Daphne was, Nicole burst into laughter.

"Daphne, I swear I'm kidding. I didn't mean to hurt your feelings."

Daphne looked at Nicole thinking this really was going to be a lousy summer.

"Listen, I'm sorry I've been so mean to you. I don't know why I was like that. But you're here now, and I don't get to hang out a lot during the summer. I just kind of figured it'd be easy to be nice to you, and maybe for the first time in my life, I might have a fun summer. Holly is nice and our families are always doing things together. I thought you're probably pretty nice too."

"Wouldn't it be fun if we made scrap books for each other and at the end of the summer we'll exchange and we'll look over all the fun stuff we did." Daphne suggested.

"It totally does, but you'll have to show me what to do, I've never done it before."

Daphne smiled and knew they had more in common than she could imagine, and maybe it was possible that they could become friends.

3

Daphne and Nicole sat in the kitchen of Nicole's house cutting out templates for scrap book pages. Daphne was excited to knit a cover for Nicole's scrapbook and leave an opening for her to put a picture of them in the middle. She was thrilled to try something new. Nicole had confided that she had been taking painting classes at the community center so she wanted paint the cover of the scrap book she'd give to Daphne.

"You know what I've always wanted to do?" Nicole asked.

"Tell me."

"I've been wanting to volunteer, like do something for the homeless people, but I'm afraid someone would see me and think I was uncool. So I've never done it."

Daphne was surprised by Nicole's confession and didn't know what to say. She was so used to being picked on all the time she couldn't imagine how it would feel to keep yourself from doing something you wanted to do because of what others thought. She realized it must take a lot of pressure to be as popular as Nicole was.

"Well, through the year I make scarves and hats and donate them to shelters in the winter. I can show you how to do it, and this winter it only takes half an hour to have someone drive us to the homeless shelter and give them away. We can do that and no one will know, and no one will think you're uncool." Nicole's face brightened, "Ok. And how about we make sandwiches to pass out to them too? How fun! And it's really nice too. And you know what else we should do!? In school, we should join a sport. Like soccer."

"Or volleyball. I've always wanted to play beach volleyball. I have no idea how they run around in the sand like that!"

They grew quiet for a moment. Daphne knew she could talk to Nicole about anything, but sometimes she still became a little nervous.

"Last night when I was walking with Holly, we were just talking, and I like her so much, but sometimes I feel like I should hate her, because then I'm being loyal to my mom. It's so confusing. I remember how through the divorce my mom was so miserable, she wouldn't leave the house, she wouldn't leave her room and I could overhear her conversations about Holly and I hated her for what she did to my family. But I know that I don't know everything and it's so hard." She looked over at Nicole who always listened, she was the best listener in the world.

"Daphne, keep taking those walks though because we need to go to the mall and get you some clothes, your pants are practically falling off of you." She said teasing Daphne by pulling them down when she stood up to get some juice.

"I thought they were becoming baggy, but you know how sometimes if you haven't washed your pants for a couple days they're baggy? I just can't keep track of them."

Nicole laughed, "How do you not keep track of your pants? What are you talking about?"

"It's just that at home I was always mixing my clothes up, and I still do but Holly does the wash and folds them and puts them on my bed, but sometimes I toss what I'm wearing on the pile before I've put them away, and then I can't remember what was what. Anyway, maybe we can go shopping the day I have my makeover?"

Holly had taken Daphne to a dermatologist who looked at her face and prescribed medicine for her. In a few short weeks, Daphne's breakouts had gone from major to minor with no scarring. Almost as quick as the acne showed up it was disappearing and she looked at her image and couldn't believe she was finally beginning to look like herself. The Daphne she'd seen all along in the mirror. With her newfound confidence she decided she'd love to get some makeup tips and had set up a makeover at Tres Belle.

Daphne's dad came into the kitchen to give her the phone and mouthed to her it was her mom on the phone. She could barely contain her excitement to speak to her mom for the first time that summer.

"Mom, I'm having so much fun! I got my hair done, and I spent half the day at the salon and felt like I was Pretty Woman, and, you'll never believe who lives next door? Nicole Gaines and we're totally becoming friends and mom, I've been walking every night with Holly and Georgie and sometimes Nicole comes and I've lost weight!" she was breathless as she waited for her mom to respond.

Daphne heard silence. "Mom are you there?"

It took a moment, but Helen finally answered, "So, you're having a good time? Is the slut trying to buy you or something?"

Tears immediately sprang to her eyes and she wasn't sure if it was because the word had hurt her so bad, or because she had instinctively become defensive of Holly. Daphne looked around to make sure no one was around; she didn't want Holly to know what had just been said.

"Mom," Daphne started in a near whisper, "How dare you say that! How dare you! She has been nothing but extraordinary to me, and I will not allow you to talk that way about her, I will no longer listen to this kind of talk."

"Oh, I see, have I been replaced?" Helen's voice cracked on the other end of the line, "first him, and now you."

"Don't be ridiculous, but I mean it mom. I want this new family, I want to be a part of it, and I am and if you have issues with dad, they're your issues not mine. I will not allow you to talk that way about Holly. I love her!" Daphne was shocked as she heard the words spill from her mouth as the tears streamed down her face. She heard her mom gasp, but Daphne said what she had to say.

"Ok Daphne. We'll have to have a serious talk when I get home because she is no role model and I might even come home early."

"Are you crazy? You sent us here and now you can't handle it. Did you really expect me to sit and pout in my room all summer, full of hate and bitterness? Is that really what you wanted for me?"

Helen was silent on the other end of the line.

"Good bye." Daphne said and hung up the phone.

She stood in silence for a moment. It was typical of her mom to not pay attention to her or listen to what she had to say, but it seemed to hurt more now than it ever had. She was grateful that Nicole had walked out when she was handed the phone but when she turned around, she noticed her dad standing in the doorway.

They looked at each other before he moved towards her and she ran into his arms. She'd been spending so much time with Holly that she suddenly felt like she had been neglecting her own father.

"Sounded like a heavy conversation." He said.

"You heard?"

"Enough." He held her tight and she felt so happy in his arms. "Honey, I'm proud that you stood up to your mom that way. I know it was hard, but we've loved you all this time. I'm glad you're growing up and are able to find a little bit of truth in what's been happening."

Daphne didn't know what to say. She wanted to relish the time she had here, at this moment in her dad's arms because she couldn't remember the last time she was in them. And for a moment, she felt as lucky as she thought Georgie was. For at that moment, her mom may have been messed up, but she did have a dad, and he smelled good too.

"Dad, you smell good." She said and looked into his face. She hadn't realized that he had brown eyes, just like her, and she was pleasantly surprised that they had the same almond shaped eyes and long eye lashes. She felt so happy to know that she actually did look like him, and to her that made him even more her father, it finally made her feel like she did fit in somewhere.

"Holly gets it for me, I have no idea what it is." He chuckled and she noted how throaty it was, like it came from deep within his soul. She suddenly felt like she didn't know him, and desperately wanted to.

"Dad, do you think we could spend some time together doing something? Just the two of us?" she asked, afraid to look at him.

"Whatever you want. You name it, we're there." He said and she felt her heart leap with joy, and little butterflies started to flit around in her stomach.

"Ok. I'll think of something." She said, still holding him tight and making sure to remember that he hadn't let go of her either.

"Thanks dad, I've got to go do my jump roping now." Daphne said as she pulled herself away.

"Yeah, you got quite a workout last night." He said as they walked out of the room.

"Oh I know! I swear I was out there jumping for an hour." She said.

He chuckled, "it was more like five minutes."

"What? Nuh uh!" she stopped in her tracks.

"Do your jump roping, it'll all pay off in the end." He said as Holly joined them.

"Hey, I forgot to tell you that my brother is coming stay with us for a few weeks." Holly said.

"Oh okay…" Daphne stammered wondering what it would be like to have so many people in the house. "What's his name?"

"Eric, he's 26, he's a musician. He's great, you're going to love him." Holly said excitedly and Daphne thought it was a little strange how enthusiastic she was, but tried not to analyze it too much.

"When is he coming?" Daphne asked.

"I'm not exactly sure, he has a really erratic and hectic schedule. Anyway, I can't wait to see him and for you to meet him." Holly said.

"Whatever." Daphne said.

Nicole walked in carrying a bag of chips and salsa and they went into Daphne's room.

When they were inside, Daphne started going over the beauty products she had on her bed.

"So this is a mask that is supposed to reduce the size of our pores and I thought we could do that. Then I thought I'd try this serum that is supposed to give your hair volume and shine."

"Ok, but lets have chips first." Nicole had already opened the bag and was munching away.

"I guess Holly has a brother who's coming to stay with us." Daphne said.

"Yeah, I heard. Eric, but you know I've never met him. And I've never heard her talk about her family much but I guess they're really close. My brother is coming home from college for a couple weeks too." Nicole said.

"You have a brother?" Daphne asked, happy to learn new information about her.

"Yeah. Robert. He's okay I guess. Just a brother."

"At least you don't have the twin brothers from hell." Daphne and Nicole sat eating chips and listening to Aquarium on the stereo.

"I want to meet Posiadyn Fisher so bad. Wouldn't it be so cool to be married to a rock star?" Daphne asked as she stared dreamily at the mural on her wall.

"I don't know if it'd be cool to marry a rock star, it'd be cool to be married to him. He's so hot." Nicole said.

"You know, this just isn't hitting the spot. I want cake." Daphne said looking at Nicole.

"That does sound good. Yum." Nicole said and they looked at each other.

"Let's see if we can make one." They jumped up and headed for the kitchen.

4

Although the expectation of Eric's arrival hung excitedly in the air, Daphne was having too much fun to care. She wasn't quite sure how it even affected her, but she promised herself to be nice whenever it was that he did show up.

The day had started out unusually fun. Nicole had spent the night, and she and Daphne and the family were in the kitchen enjoying breakfast. Daphne loved Sunday breakfasts with her family because they would make omelets and watching her dad with Holly in the kitchen was always full of sarcasm and wit, as they lovingly teased each other. Daphne looked around the table at everyone but her mind wandered to a time when there were no family breakfasts, she didn't get along with her brothers and rarely talked to her mom. Now almost everyday was full of laughter and fun and she felt herself get choked up at the thought of it ending.

A crash could be heard and everyone turned to Ritchie who was standing in the doorway with a plate in his hand.

"Sorry Holly. I broke the plate, but a limo just pulled up in front of our house."

Holly grinned as she looked over to Todd.

"A limo?" Daphne asked. She exchanged glances with Nicole and without hesitation they both leaped out of their chairs.

"Are you sure it's a limo?" Nicole asked.

"I know what a limo is." Ritchie said sarcastically.

Nicole and Daphne exchanged glances as they stood on the porch waiting to see who would emerge from the limo.

"Oh, I guess my brother is here." Holly said nonchalantly.

"Is he rich or something?" Daphne asked trying to get a good look.

A couple kids had run over and were standing by the limo while a kid on a bike rode over. A small crowd was beginning to gather.

Daphne laughed. "You'd think you're brother was famous or something Holly. Look at the crowds! Any minute and you'd think the paparazzi would be here."

"Oh they'll be here soon enough." Holly said as she moved out from behind them and started to walk towards the limo with Georgie in her arms.

Daphne, Nicole, Ryan and Ritchie followed.

The door opened and they still couldn't see anything. Then a foot emerged.

"Dad, is that really Holly's brother?" Daphne asked as she turned to face her father.

"Yeah, we told you he was coming." Daphne was looking at her dad when she heard Nicole gasp.

"No way!" she shrieked and Daphne turned to look at her friend who was visibly shaking.

"Nicole, calm down..." her voice trailed as she followed Nicole's gaze and finally caught a glimpse of the man who had just stepped from the limo.

She watched as all 6 glorious feet of the beautiful Posiadyn Fisher bent down to hug Holly. She watched him take Georgie and remark at how cute she was. It suddenly got very loud as the kids started shouting, camera phones were going off in every direction, she could hear girls screaming and see more kids running over and people walking down the street towards the house.

Daphne felt like everything was happening in slow motion and she suddenly lost a little bit of her sense of reality. She felt herself getting a little disoriented as she took in the scene before her. Kids were screaming for Posiadyn Fisher, and there he was a few feet away from her hugging her step mom. It was like a poster of him was standing in front of her and she wasn't quite sure what was going on.

She looked at Nicole whose face looked as confused as hers. Daphne looked at her dad who was looking back at her with a smile on his face.

"Oh my god, Daph, do you get it?" Nicole asked her as she took her by the arms and turned her so that they were face to face.

"Posiadyn Fisher is Holly's brother!" They screamed in unison and then the reality of the situation finally hit Daphne and she started to jump up and down. She couldn't help it, tears started rolling down her face and she stood there waiting for the moment to be introduced to him as she hung onto Nicole for dear life.

Holly walked over, Posiadyn Fisher behind her and holding Georgie.

"These are the twins, Ryan and Ritchie, Nicole who is Tammy's daughter, and here is my step daughter who I told you all about, Daphne."

Daphne could feel her heart stop as she met his intense, blue eyes and could see him smile at her. She told herself to remember the moment forever. He handed the baby to Todd and bent down to hug Daphne.

"I've heard a lot about you. I'm happy to finally meet you."

She felt his arms around her, better than any dream she'd ever had, and couldn't believe that it was real and this was really happening to her. She thought he had held her forever and he looked at her and the words couldn't come out of her mouth. She felt her mouth open, but nothing.

Kids started to swarm around him.

"Can I have your autograph?" she heard it coming from every direction. "Where's the rest of the band", "What are you doing here?" and she could see phones pointed in her direction and lights flashing and for a brief moment, she knew what it would be like to be a celebrity.

Posiadyn politely turned to them and with more charm than she could have imagined, he said, "you know what guys, can you come back later and I can talk with you and sign stuff, right now I'd just like to spend time with my family," He turned away from the crowd, took Daphne's hand and put his other arm around Holly and led the family into the house. Her heart was racing, she was actually holding hands with Posiadyn Fisher!

Once inside everyone was talking at once Holly and Posiadyn were catching up, the twins were running around, Georgie toddling around chasing after the barking dogs, Nicole and Daphne sat on the couch, in silence and awe.

"Is that really him?" Daphne leaned her face near Nicole's without her eyes leaving his face.

Both girls were still in shock, that Posiadyn Fisher, rock star, hot guy, Holly's brother! Was in their living room.

"It looks like him." Nicole whispered back.

Nicole and Daphne sat so close on the couch, you couldn't get a piece of paper between them. Holly glanced in their direction and chuckled.

"What do you think?" Holly asked, directing her question to Daphne.

Daphne and Nicole just grinned.

"Pretty big surprise huh Daph?" her dad asked.

Daphne nodded her head.

"Are you really Posiadyn Fisher?" Nicole asked.

"Yes, but call me Eric." He said his voice smooth and low, and Daphne felt tingles go up and down her body.

"Why? Isn't your name Posiadyn?" asked Ritchie.

"It's a stage name." Todd said to Ritchie.

"Do you have a girlfriend?" Ryan asked.

"No, not right now." He replied.

"Daphne wants to marry you." Ritchie said.

"Ritchie!" Daphne screeched as she sunk further down into the sofa.

"So are you going to make a brother starve or what? I could use some grub." Posiadyn said, finally sitting on a chair in the living room as he reached into a leather bag that had been placed by it. Daphne had remembered seeing the short driver bringing bags in but she was in such a daze she hadn't been paying attention.

"Todd is probably getting the grill fired up right now. He's gone all out landscaping the backyard, turning it into his backyard bar, he'll love to show it all to you." Holly rolled her eyes.

Nicole and Daphne continued to stare.

"Hey girls, you can close your mouths now. It really is me." Posiadyn said and the girls could finally break free of a giggle.

"What are you doing here anyway? Don't you have a tour? Or music videos to shoot or an appearance on TRL?" Nicole asked.

Posiadyn laughed again. Daphne made sure to note that he seemed to be eternally amused. Almost as eternally amused as Holly was eternally chipper. Was there something wrong with them?

"I have a little down time right now. Our album was released last year and we're finished touring for now. We do have a video shoot scheduled and we're performing at the MTV music awards." He said.

Daphne couldn't hold in her delight as she squealed.

"I can bring you guys if you'd like." He offered.

"What?" they both asked in unison.

"I'll just call my manager. You can come, be my dates. Here I have a couple things for you." He brought out a couple gift bags and handed one to Nicole and one to Daphne. Inside were t-shirts from their concert tour. The front of it was a picture of the whole band with the tour dates listed on back. Daphne was so excited to receive it that the fact it was a size to small didn't matter, better to hang it on her wall then to wear it and it become faded.

Daphne and Nicole looked at each other, and Daphne couldn't help it. She burst into tears.

"Daph?" Holly asked.

Daphne just shook her head and covered her face with her hands. Nicole put her arm around her.

Posiadyn shot a concerned look at Holly.

"I think she's probably in shock Eric. You're not a fantasy to her anymore. You're a live person standing before her eyes and you just fulfilled one of her dearest dreams by being real, then you add to that, you just invited her to something she's only seen on TV. She's a teenager, she's overwhelmed." Holly said as he went to the sofa and sat on the other side of Daphne.

He took her hand in his and put his arm around her trying to shift her weight from leaning on Nicole to leaning on him.

"Daphne. I am a person just like you. I have a sister, you know my niece better than I do, and your dad is my brother-in-law. You didn't know any of that before today, but I'd say I'm pretty real. It's great to have fans, but they sometimes put us in this stratosphere where we're no longer human beings, but celebrities. Celebrity isn't all it's cracked up to be if I can't get close to people is it?"

Daphne listened to him speak, her face still buried in her hands as her head rested against his chest.

She was confused. Thoughts and emotions she'd never felt before were running through her head and she felt dizzy.

She finally lifted her head. Her face red, and hot, she could feel beads of sweat on her forehead.

"I'm good with words when you're a poster on my wall. When you're on my wall, you're an equal. When you stand here in front of me, you're real, as real as anyone who's ever let me down." She couldn't believe that she was able to put what she was feeling into words.

"Ah," he said, "well, I won't let you down as long as you don't have unrealistic expectations of me. How's that?"

"What do you mean?" Daphne asked.

"Forget that I'm Posiadyn Fisher. Just think of me as Eric, your step mom's brother. Step mom, weird huh Holly?' he said and laughed at Holly who rolled her eyes, "let's not think about videos, and MTV and tours and we won't buy any gossip magazines. We'll go camping and travel and go to dinner and do all things that families do…"

"And try to forget that the paparazzi are following our every move." Nicole interrupted.

"Anyway, that's where you start Daphne. When I'm with you here, in this house with our family, I'm Eric. It'll be easier than you think." He squeezed her and she felt comforted.

Eric, Posiadyn? She was very confused, but whoever it was sitting next to her, she definitely liked him. She thought he was nice and friendly and he was an adult who didn't talk down to her or tell her what to do. He was likeable and when she thought of him like that, for a moment she could forget he was Posiadyn Fisher. That was when she wasn't looking at him. Then she would turn and look into his sparkling blue eyes, and that smile with his full bottom lip, and there went the tingles and butterflies in her stomach that up to that point she'd only experienced in dreams she'd have of him. As he sat next to her, she knew that reality was that she was fourteen and he was in his twenties, and they wouldn't get married, and she wouldn't be his groupie and was she okay with having to let go of those dreams? As a poster, she could still have daydreams. Daydreams were way more possible than reality. Daydreams didn't let her down.

"The only thing I know for sure is that I feel like my dreams all became very complicated." Daphne said.

Everyone was quiet.

"Well, I'm going home for a sec, I've got to tell my mom that you're here, *Eric*, and then we'll come back." Nicole said and she bent down and kissed Daphne on the cheek. "It's going to be the best summer of our lives Daph! Wait and see."

Posiadyn/Eric said goodbye to Nicole and continued to hold Daphne's hand.

"Are you okay now?" he asked.

"Yeah, I'm going to go in my room for a little bit." She said as she jumped off the couch, she couldn't look at him and instead she hurried out of the living room.

Once inside her room, Daphne sat against her door blocking it from opening. She didn't want anyone to come in. She was confused and wanted to be alone for a little while. She wanted to knit. She reached over to her knitting bag and took out the sky blue scarf she'd been working on. It was for Posiadyn Fisher of all people, she thought to herself. Her plan was to mail it to him as a gift. A feeling of giddiness overcame her as she realized she could give it to him herself. She looked at the mural of him on her wall. Where he was once bigger than life, now he was real, and somewhere in the house that was on the other side of the door she sat in front of. Honestly, she didn't know if she liked the idea of him being so close to her. He was a huge part of her life now, something that couldn't be taken away. He was her step mom's brother. Did that make him her uncle? It certainly wasn't normal to have feelings for your uncle. She was in trouble for sure. Her dreams of scrap booking their tour stops, walking down the red carpet with him...if they all came true, what would she dream of next? Would she die if all her dreams came true? What happens when you have all that you ever wanted? Her nerves started to stand on end a little. She'd have to make a mental note of all the things she's ever dreamed of, to make sure she'd have enough to take her to 15, then 16, and then at least to 18...anything past 18 seemed way too far away.

As her needles clicked together and the scarf became longer, out of habit she was still talking to her mural. Her conversation was interrupted when Holly came in her room.

"We're going out to dinner to celebrate my brother coming home. Come downstairs when you're ready." Holly smiled.

As she looked at Holly, Daphne wondered if she'd ever reach the happiness that Holly seemed to have. Daphne could think of no adults...not her mom, not her teachers, cashiers at the store, no adults that exuded as much warmth and kindness as Holly. Holly was perky, she was nice, and she had a smile for everyone. She was charming and always had something nice to say. She had so much love for everyone she met and also seemed to want to give to others. She was often curious as to how someone as fun as Holly could be seen as so bad in her mother's eyes.

As Daphne looked at the clothes that hung in her closet, she realized she was collecting a wardrobe. In the short time since she'd been staying with her dad, she'd acquired more jeans, shorts, a ton of tops, shoes, underclothes; she actually had clothes to choose from. What would she wear in the presence of Posiadyn Fisher? Eric, she reminded herself.

Eric. She whispered as she took her makeup bag and sat on her bed applying the makeup she learned to wear from her makeover. Still trying to decide what to wear she wondered what Holly would wear. Something pink for sure. Daphne wanted to be like Holly. Happy, and with a life and she felt like she was on her way.

Daphne had a lot of clothes now, but still couldn't sway from her comfy jeans and a bulky hoody. She and Nicole had ordered hoodies online and although Nicole wouldn't be joining them for dinner, by wearing their twin hoody she'd be there in spirit. Nicole. Once upon a time the girl wouldn't look at her in the hallways and now they were practically best friends. She didn't know what had changed Nicole's mind about wanting to be her friend, but now she couldn't imagine summer and what's beyond without her.

Daphne knew she really was changing when she chose her "crafty jeans" to wear out in public. Her creations she would wear only in the comfort of her home where she knew no one would say anything about them. On her "crafty jeans" she had glued crystals to the back pockets of her jeans, on the left pocket her initial, a "D", and the right pocket, a daisy; a little something to individualize them and make them her own. Her accessory du jour was a comfortable, worn in pair of flip flops that she had glued crystals to the straps. She liked to make her clothes bling and loved the way the light reflected off crystals. She put them on everything she wore to make them unlike anything anyone else was wearing. She knew that although everyone in the world could be hot gluing crystals to their clothes no two things would ever be the same. This summer, around her dad and Holly, and her new friend Nicole, she was beginning to feel comfortable in her clothes and was excited to be seen out wearing them. She also figured that her creations were the only thing that could make her feel even a fraction as fabulous as she should feel to be seen with Posiadyn Fisher.

Daphne looked at herself in the mirror. She almost didn't recognize herself. She was happy with her hair, it looked healthy, and the cut really suited her. Her makeup looked great, and she could see in her face that she'd lost weight. She could distinctly make out her neck and her chin had a little point. Her face had cleared up from the medication a dermatologist gave her. She didn't feel like her clothes looked trendy, but the personal touches she added to her jeans and flip flops made her feel like she may have some style.

"Me?" she said to herself in the mirror... "Do I have style?" she grinned and walked out of her room.

In the living room they were all waiting for her. She looked first at Posiadyn/ Eric she reminded herself yet again, and then looked away.

"Cute jeans Daph, maybe you can add those crystals to my jeans too?" Holly smile and Daphne nodded.

They stood for a moment before her dad prompted them outside. A limo waited for them at the sidewalk in front of the house.

"Yeah, we're riding in the limo" Ryan squealed.

"Aww right!" Ritchie said as he and Ryan raced to the limo.

"We're taking a limo to the restaurant?" Daphne asked.

She tried to contain her excitement, but she couldn't. She felt tears spring to her eyes as she slid in behind her brothers. The inside of the limo was nothing like she could have imagined. The seats looked like leather and were in the shape of a U. She slid in as far as she could and noticed a mini bar and a small television which was encased in a mini entertainment center that held several different video game systems. She noticed a sun roof and envisioned herself hanging out of it like she'd seen on so many television shows and movies where the girls are all beautiful and dressed up and screaming at the top of their lungs.

She wiped the tears from her eyes and hoped that her makeup wasn't smeared. Holly slid in next to her and noticed her wiping away her tears.

"Sweetie, what's wrong?" she asked and put her arm around Daphne.

"I just can't believe I'm in a limo. I didn't think I'd ever in my life get to ride in a limo." Daphne said, feeling herself wanting to cry more as she spoke.

"Well, now you're in a limo. It's nice huh?" Holly said.

"Yeah." Daphne was in awe and didn't know what else to say or how she could explain what was going through her mind. She felt like she had won one of those contests where you win back stage passes and get a chance to meet your favorite band. She'd often dreamed if Aquarium had come to her town, that she would win one of those contests and finally get to meet Posiadyn Fisher. Only this was no contest. This whole experience was real and she'd get more than a few hours to be in the presence of someone she'd only dreamt about. She practically laughed out loud at how drastically things had changed in an afternoon. Whereas once her dream was to get a glance of him in person, or win a contest just to see him in person, now he sat a few people away from her and would be staying in her house for weeks. They were connected for life!

"Can we play those video games?" Ritchie asked.

"Are you sure you want to start? You'll have to stop when we get to the restaurant." Todd said.

"That's ok. We can stop." Ryan said.

When they pulled up outside the restaurant Daphne's heart

sank. Daphne had driven by this restaurant several times with her mom and she always said it looked so fancy and she dreamed of going in. Daphne seemed to be doing a lot of things her mom wished to do, and she was doing them with someone her mom didn't like. Daphne was in another situation where her loyalty to her mother felt challenged. She hesitated getting out. She hated having experiences that she knew her mother dreamed about and didn't have the opportunity to do them. She was excited that her world was opening up in such a way that she was able to experience what it was like to have a life that existed beyond sitting in a room talking to posters and knitting, but what about her mom?

"Come on." Eric said to her as he bent down to see why she was still in the limo. He reached his hand out to her, and she was mesmerized by his smile and slid out of the limo.

People were looking at them as they walked into the restaurant and Daphne tried to ignore the stares. There were people sitting in the corridor, obviously waiting to get in and eat, but they went straight in and Daphne wondered if it was because they were with a celebrity. She expected to be seated at "the finest" table, or the table that was in the middle where everyone could see them.

Instead, they were shown to a simple table, towards the back and in a corner.

"Your server will be here in a moment." The maitre d said and smiled.

"Is this the finest table here?" Daphne whispered. There was something about the candle light that made her think she had to be quiet.

"No." Eric laughed. "When we made the reservation we asked to be seated away from the crowd so we could enjoy our meal."

"Because people will ask us for pictures and autographs huh?" Ryan asked.

"They will anyway it happens all the time, but back here we'll go unnoticed a little longer." Eric said.

They all sat and Daphne looked at her menu. She wasn't one for fine dining, but knew if the prices weren't on the menu, they were more than what she could imagine.

She felt herself get a little queasy and excused herself to go to the bathroom.

In the bathroom she locked herself in a stall and let the tears flow. She wasn't choking down sobs, but she was sniffling a lot and when she heard the toilet flush she sucked in her breath hoping the person who just flushed didn't hear a thing.

Daphne heard the water running, the dispenser being pushed and then she heard some heels clack against the floor and the door open and close. Daphne blew her nose and thought it was probably best for her to try composing herself, but the tears kept coming. She heard the clacking again and than a soft tap on her stall door.

"Are you okay in there?" it was a soft, pretty voice whose accent echoed through the bathroom.

Daphne was confused. Did that trickster toilet flusher only pretend to leave the bathroom? "I'm fine." Daphne croaked out.

"Do you need me to get your mom?" the pretty voice asked.

"No, oh no, I'm okay. I uh…I…" Daphne stammered and didn't know what to say, so she opened the stall door.

Standing by the door was a really cute woman. She was tall, she had short red hair that reminded her of pictures of Princess Diana's hair she'd seen in books her mom had. She looked at Daphne with concern in her brown eyes.

"Why aren't you a pretty thang? Why are you crying like that in such a lovely restaurant?" the woman took a wash cloth that was on the counter by the sink and ran it under the water and handed it to Daphne.

"I don't even know where to start." Daphne took the wash cloth and tried carefully to wipe under her eyes without wiping all her makeup off.

"Well, I'm listenin." The woman said and she lifted herself on the counter. "But first, tell me your name."

"Daphne."

"Good to meet you Daphne, I'm Jane. I'm all ears."

"Well, I'm here with my step mom who my mom hates, and I feel bad because my mom always talks about coming here because it's so fancy and nice and she can't afford to come here because of me and my brothers, but here I am and I feel like I shouldn't be here without her and I feel weird. And to top it off, Posiadyn Fisher is sitting right out there. At my table. Sitting right next to me." She took a breath when it was all out.

"Hold up Daphne, you're here with Posiadyn Fisher?" Jane's eyes widened with excitement.

"You know Posiadyn Fisher?" Daphne giggled.

"Of course I do. I have a girl about your age. He's here, with you?" she asked again.

"Yeah, and it's totally freaking me out, like his name is Eric and I cant stop calling him Posiadyn and it's all just a weird sloppy mess and I can't stop crying." Daphne said. Talking about it was calming her down.

Jane was thoughtful for a moment, not taking her eyes off Daphne's face once.

"Hm...well baby, I don't know what to tell you. But because I'm a momma I can say this. Your momma would want the best for you, if you're here, enjoy it double. Once for you and once for her. I know you're feelin all weird, it sounds like you've been swept up by some extraordinary events. But just try to remember that Posiadyn Fisher is just a boy, like you're a girl, he's just a person, here with his family and trying to have a normal life like everyone else. He's handsome and talented and you're getting an opportunity that not many people get, you're meetin your idol. So enjoy it because if there's one thang I know for sure, it's that life will become normal again before you know it, and you'll miss the days you had with him and you'll only remember wasting the time by crying it all away. So wipe that pretty face of yours, smile and have a great time! The food here is ta die for and you'll have some exciting tales to share with your momma."

Daphne looked at her, hoping she understood what Jane was trying to say, but she was so in love with her accent that she was about to ask her to repeat herself but thought it might be rude.

"Thanks Jane," was all she could get out.

"Do you think you could get his autograph for me?" Jane asked, and then laughed a musical laugh that reverberated off the walls. "I'm kiddin baby. I have to get back out to my date. But remember what I said. Just have fun." She took Daphne by the hand and they opened the bathroom door.

All eyes were on Daphne when she reached the table. Averting her eyes from Eric, she sat down.

"The waiter came, I ordered you a steak ok, Daph?" her dad asked.

"Yeah, that sounds good, you know what I like."

Once the food started arriving, and Daphne noticed that her dad, Holly and Eric started drinking a little, the conversation turned lively and she soon forgot the trauma of being there without her mom.

Eric held everyone's attention as he shared stories of touring with different bands. She liked the insider knowledge he was sharing about how they would book their rooms under their real names and the little bit of privacy they were able to get doing it that way. With the exception of his mom who often tipped the tabloids as to his whereabouts or if he was seeing anyone new. She was a little bit of a limelight hog, and also enjoyed the fact that her son was famous and the perks she sometimes got for being associated with him. He talked about being friends with celebrities and the craziness in Los Angeles. She was dying to know who he was talking about when he said he was linked in the tabloids to a supermodel who he never actually met in real life, but when they did they hooked up but she turned into a complete psychotic and obsessed groupie who would show up backstage at several of his shows. He talked about being on the road and how fun the fans were and how a little girl he met with leukemia inspired his song "Heart of Soul" because she was so smart and passionate but died at only ten years old. He talked about partying and the trashed motel room rumors and how press made it into a circus,

"We'll be working on a video soon, I'm wondering if you'd like to go to L.A. with me and be in it Daphne." Eric asked.

Daphne almost choked on her food. "Are you kidding me?" she asked as she drank some water to make her food go down.

"No, I'm not kidding," Eric chuckled, "I'll get back to you about the dates. But it will be soon."

Todd looked at Daphne and smiled.

"What would I do?" Daphne asked.

"We're not quite sure yet. It's a toss up about which single we'll do next, and once we do decide, when we find the director and get ideas, then we'll know. But I'm sure we could use you." Eric flashed her his super star smile and she felt the heat color her cheeks.

"Did I tell you how great you looked honey?" her dad asked.

"No." she giggled, as the heat grew hotter on her face. She felt like her family must be on a mission to embarrass her.

All that was happening around her was a wonder to Daphne. She glanced around at all the people, the light conversation, laughter and clinking of silverware against plates and ice against glass was music to her ears. The restaurant was rather dark, with low lighting on the ceiling and the glow of the small candles that were the centerpieces on each table. And the food, like Jane said, "was ta die for", she couldn't remember the last time she'd tasted such a juicy steak. She swiped a steak fry in the juice from her steak and tried to remember what Jane had told her in the bathroom about her mom. Daphne was trying to remember every little detail to share with her mom. Daphne's own feelings had changed regarding Holly but she knew that didn't mean her mom would be ready, or as willing to accept her.

Her mom was so bitter, and angry. Daphne had no idea what it would be like to be married and then get divorced, but what she did know was that eventually you'd move on. Daphne wasn't sure her mom had done that. Throughout the summer it was becoming apparent that the semester at sea program was a blessing in disguise because Daphne's life had certainly taken a turn she'd never expect. Hopefully the same thing was happening for her mom.

After dinner when they took the limo home, everyone changed into their pajamas and gathered around in the living room to watch movies. Daphne liked sitting on the overstuffed couch, next to her dad who sat with her baby sister on his lap. The twins lying on sleeping bags on the floor and Eric sitting in the big chair. It felt comfortable; it felt like a home to have bodies all over the place, just being together. When Daphne was home, she was often locked in her room because her brothers horded the TV with their video games. If her mom wasn't grading homework, she was passed out early in her room. Now that Daphne had something to compare it too, she sure didn't have much of a home life when she was back home. She was resolved to make a new life for herself when she got back there.

When Georgie fell asleep, Holly and her dad took her to put her to bed and called it a night. The boys had fallen asleep on the floor and it left only her and Eric in the living room. She wanted so desperately to talk to him, and get to know him, but she didn't know what to say, or where to start. As if he was reading her mind, he started the conversation with her by asking her about school. She told him how the kids picked on her and how she didn't feel like she fit in and desperately wanted too, especially for high school. She loved math and history, and art, but hated English and P.E. She talked about how Holly took her to get her hair done and makeup and took her shopping and how she was becoming a new person. She was surprised how easy it was to talk to him, and how she couldn't believe her own willingness to tell him about things that made her uncomfortable. She told him about her mom and how much she disliked Holly, how she started out wanting to hate her and now she couldn't. Daphne told him about her dreams of maybe being a scarf designer. How she once dreamed of going on tour with him and scrap booking her adventures. She told him how she loved to redesign her own clothes and maybe she might want to study fashion and if they didn't have a knitting club at her new high school she would start one. And she loved how he sat there and listened and laughed with her and never ridiculed her or her dreams and how easy it was being with him when she forgot he was Posiadyn Fisher.

"What about you. Did you always want to be famous? Did you ever imagine you'd be Posiadyn Fisher?" she asked him.

He told her he'd been writing music, singing and playing instruments as long as he could remember. He was such a passionate and vivid storyteller that when he told her the story about getting his first Fisher Price guitar when he was five, she felt like she was sitting there with him on the green sofa when his dad handed it to him. When he was in high school and was jilted by a girl he was in love with and that's when he decided he had to be famous because he had to prove to her that he was someone special. She could almost see the dumb girl's brown hair teased on top and the sides and wondered what he could really see in someone with such bad hair anyway. She even almost lost her concentration imagining him really liking someone with mall hair. She got lost with him when he told her about the thrill of getting his first contract after singing in small bars and borrowing money from his grandparents to put together his first demo tape, she was reliving his excitement with him. Eric explained to her that although he had no idea they would become as famous as they were, that he had it set in his mind that his life would never be the same and that he would ride the wave wherever it took him. He tried to explain that although he may be famous, he was still the same person he was in high school who struggled to make demo tapes hoping that his music would get that girls attention and it never did.

"How weird, what kind of girl would still ignore you after all that you've accomplished?" she asked.

"I don't know." He said. "Maybe a small town girl who really can't get her heart to grasp something bigger than herself. Maybe the type of girl who couldn't leave the comfort of her mother's bosom…" Eric trailed off.

He jumped up, "Hold on." He said and he came back writing in a long, skinny notebook that she'd seen reporters use.

"What are you doing?" she asked.

"I'm writing lyrics down, this is inspiring stuff." He chuckled and she started knitting while he wrote a new song.

5

Daphne didn't do bright and early very well, but that's exactly what it was the morning Nicole came pounding on the front door excited that her brother was coming home.

Daphne full of crankiness and still trying to get the eye boogies out of her eyes sleepily shuffled through the house to plop on the couch.

Holly was up and bright as a sunray feeding Georgie and Eric was making omelets in the kitchen.

Omelets? She couldn't stifle her giddiness as she went into the kitchen to make sure she wasn't dreaming. There he stood, hair still damp from his shower, wearing a pair of jeans and white t-shirt as he chopped onions and tomatoes while the sweet smell of bacon fried in a pan.

"I still can't believe Posiadyn Fisher is staying in this house." Daphne giggled as she and Nicole headed back out into the living room.

"Eric. His name is Eric." Nicole reminded her.

"Oh right." Daphne yawned, "So, 7 am. Girl! I need my sleep."

"Oh my god! I'm so excited for you to meet my brother! I

haven't seen him in so long. He won't even be here that long, but anyway." Nicole trailed off.

"I'm just tired. What time is he coming in?" Daphne said, not lifting her head from the arm of the couch.

"I don't know. Whenever he gets here." A ring interrupted Nicole's sentence and she paused to answer her cell phone.

"Hiiiiiii!" she squealed into the phone and mouthed to Daphne that her brother was on the phone. "uh huh…ok…ohmagod! Ok…" Daphne couldn't help but laugh. She'd never seen Nicole act so goofy. Nicole was the girl too cool to respond, too cool to be seen as anyone other than the observer. With the exception of Posiadyn Fisher showing up in a limousine, you were allowed to freak out when your dream guy shows up in your front yard.

"Nicole do you want to stay for breakfast?" Holly wandered in, Georgie toddling behind her who climbed onto Daphne's lap.

"Sure, what's on the menu?" Nicole asked.

"Omelets, hash browns, toast, freshly squeezed orange juice." Holly sounded like a commercial.

"Are you kidding me? Did he actually squeeze the oranges?" Daphne asked.

"Yes he did."

Nicole and Daphne giggled and ran into the kitchen. They sat at the table, chins in their hands as they watched Eric scramble eggs and toss handfuls of cheese, onions and other toppings in the omelets.

"I can't believe you can cook. When do you have time?" Nicole asked incredulously.

"Well," Eric said as he studied the flame under the pan and Nicole and Daphne exchanged glances, "when you live on the road for months on end and live on fast food and diner food, sometimes you just want to have a home cooked meal."

"Plus all the drinking and the partying." Nicole added.

Holly frowned and Eric shot her a look while he continued watching the omelet. "Well Nicole, there is some of that, but the partying isn't my scene. Just like everything else it can get old."

"What about groupies?" Nicole asked.

Daphne couldn't help but laugh out loud and Eric and Holly both looked at Nicole.

"What is with you this morning?" Holly asked.

"I think I want to be a reporter and find the dirty truth about life on the road as a rocker." Nicole said very matter-of-factly.

Daphne shook her head and rolled her eyes. The Nicole she loved who wasn't afraid to speak her mind and ask ridiculous questions.

"Anyway..." Eric said, "Here you go." As he placed in front of them two plates with the most beautiful looking omelets Daphne had ever seen complete with orange slices and a green sprig of something as a garnish. She was sorry she didn't have a camera to take their picture and send it in to a food magazine with a caption that said, "Posiadyn Fisher cooks!".

"What is this?" Nicole asked as she lifted the herb to her nose.

"Mint" Eric said.

Daphne bit into her omelet as Eric looked at her expectantly. She nodded with a grin as she tasted the buttery egg and the perfectly melted cheese, bacon bits and onions to top off the perfect bite.

"Taste my hash browns." He ordered Daphne.

"Did you make these from scratch or are they from a bag?" she asked.

"They're mine, I shredded the potatoes myself, tossed them with some onion and garlic in the pan." He said.

"Oh my god! They are delicious!" Nicole exclaimed as Daphne nodded in agreement.

Even the orange juice was the tastiest and most flavorful juice full of pulpy bits that she'd ever tasted.

"There certainly is something to be said for fresh ingredients." Daphne said as she watched Eric continue cooking.

"This is really good food. Did you train in Paris or something?" Nicole asked as she gobbled her omelet down.

"You might want to slow down Nicole, I mean you're going to choke." Daphne laughed

"Just practice a lot. I cook whenever I get the chance." He said.

A rock star who's nice, and cooks, and cute, and writes songs... Daphne's crush wasn't disappearing, it was getting bigger. He'd even made Georgie a mini-omelet of her own and kissed her on her forehead as he set it in front of her on her high chair.

Nicole and Daphne looked at each other and swooned.

"Ok guys... Eric, thank you so much for the omelet." Nicole stood up and excitedly headed to the door, "Gonna go wait for my brother, Holly you know barbecue our place right?"

"We'll be there sweets." Holly smiled. Nicole blew Daphne a kiss and skipped out.

"Eric, what was the girl's name anyway?" Daphne asked a little embarrassed and hoping he couldn't tell that she'd been obsessing about it since the night he told her.

"Frankie. Her name was Frankie Casserini. I think it was short for Francesca, I can't remember. She was a hottie. Broke my heart." He said as he continued to cook and she got the impression he was over her and she had nothing to worry about anymore. The phone rang and Daphne ran to answer it because she was expecting to hear from her mom.

"Hi mom!" Daphne said excitedly as she heard her mom's voice. "You are not going to believe this! Guess who is here and just made me an omelet good enough to drive the Gods to give up their diets. Posiadyn Fisher!" Daphne looked at Eric who smiled at her. "Only his name is really Eric and he is Holly's brother! No I'm not kidding...no! Mom..." the excitement drained from her body and she could see Holly roll her eyes and Daphne decided to take the call in the other room.

Daphne was quieted as she listened to her mom bad mouth Holly and the disbelief that Eric and Posiadyn Fisher was the same person. She knew Holly had a brother named Eric but why wouldn't her father have mentioned that he happened to be a famous musician. Daphne felt sadness fill her stomach as she decided not to mention the fancy restaurant. Daphne was so full of disappointment that she didn't even know what to say. All her smart mouth comebacks left her mind as her excitement disappeared too.

"Yes mom, yes, they've taken me to the orthodontist. Yes the boys are eating their veggies. Everything is fine mom." Daphne couldn't wait to get her mom off the phone. "Yes I'm curious as to how your trip is mom but you're too busy bitching you haven't told me about it yet. Sorry mom, sorry, sorry...no mom I'm not allowed to cuss it just came out...no mom there are not groupies and weirdoes stalking the house...ok mom, listen I have to get in the shower. The boys are still sleeping...they'll be up soon. Ok, love you too." Daphne hung up the phone and had to take a deep breath to get over the drama. She was positive there would never be peace between her mom and Holly. Her mom could find no good in anything Holly said or did. She thought there was a hidden motive to everything Holly did. The motive was to make her mom's life a living hell. Daphne sometimes wondered if her mom was paranoid. What was wrong with her mom that she could hang onto so much hatefulness? Why couldn't her mom just get over it? Daphne looked at Eric, who had a sympathetic look on his face, but she was too embarrassed to stay, she had to be alone in her room.

In the quiet of her room Daphne sat on her bed. There was an ache along her back and she twisted her body from side to side to try to release the tension that was creeping its way through her bones. She had been so happy and suddenly she just wanted to put her head down and go back to sleep. Couldn't her mom for one minute just listen to what Daphne had to say and be happy for her? She looked around the room she was falling in love with. The room that was orderly and clean and had beautiful things. The lovely quilt that Holly had made for her, all her fun make up and an actual wardrobe. Daphne knew in her heart that when she left at the end of the summer she would be leaving more than her beautiful things behind. She'd be leaving behind a lifestyle, a way of life. A life where impossible dreams could actually be a reality and where love and laughter existed more than negativity and loneliness. Her mom would freak if she saw all the nice clothes that her dad could afford when her mom scraped by. As Daphne looked at how she looked in the mirror, she wondered if her mom would even be happy at the weight she had lost. She no longer had the gut hanging over her pants, she had a flat stomach and her double chin had disappeared. Daphne could glimpse herself back home: eating all the time and getting no exercise. Just like before. She could see herself hiding in her room and as the misery helped her pack on the weight she began to wonder if with every pound she packed back on would Nicole take a step back? Daphne tried to tell herself that wouldn't happen. It only took a moment for insecurity to fill her up and tears start to stream down her face. She didn't want to leave her dad's house. She wanted to stay there forever. How could she manage that?

Her dad had gone to work and she'd have to wait all day for him to get home. When Daphne finished her shower and had dressed, she didn't go back out to the living room. She was too sad. She sat on her floor in the room, knitting in front of the mural.

There was a knock on the door and Daphne knew it was Holly, who slowly opened the door.

"Hey, what happened to you?" Holly asked as she sat down next to Daphne.

Daphne put her knitting down and sighed. She looked at the mural and didn't know where to begin. She still wasn't quite sure what she could share with Holly, and the last thing she wanted to do was hurt her feelings.

"I guess the conversation didn't go so well with your mom?" Holly asked.

Daphne took a moment. "You know what I'm most afraid of? That all the magic of this summer will disappear forever when I leave to go back home. I'm going to put weight back on, I'll lose Nicole as a friend, and I'll only have posters of Posiadyn Fisher on the walls of my cluttered room. It'll be over. It'll all be gone." Tears started to stream down her face.

Holly put her arm around Daphne. "I like the idea that you look at this as magic, but it's all very real Daphne. Eric will always be your friend, you'll always be welcome here. I'll come pick you up if you want to walk, Nicole will be your friend forever. Daph, your life is different now and once a life changes, it's never the same again. Maybe if you'd like we can go to your house and fix your room up. I'm sure you have the key. Don't cry sweetie. I will not let you be unhappy anymore."

"It's my mom. She just makes me unhappy." Daphne sighed, ashamed that she had said it out loud.

"I don't know what to say about Helen. I've tried, we've tried to be amicable with her and she won't have it. Listen Daphne, I need to tell you something." Holly sighed and Daphne knew something big was coming. "It is really important to me that you know the truth about me and your dad. You're old enough to talk to about this. The first thing is that your dad and I were not having an affair. I can understand your mom thinking that but the truth is that we were simply colleagues. You know he was the architect and he knew me by reputation and we'd collaborated on projects together and would refer me to his clients when they wanted consultations. We knew each other for awhile. We didn't speak about our private lives when we worked together, it was very professional. Because we had a working relationship your mom assumed stuff happened that never happened. Your dad was out of the house, the divorce finalized the first time he asked me out. He had that little apartment out by The Ranch remember? So I knew he wasn't trying to seduce me, or be a bad guy. He was lonely and hurting and we became friends."

Holly paused for a minute, Daphne could hear the tremble in her voice as her eyes became watery, "And I fell in love with him. I mean, your dad…" she giggled, "besides being fantastically handsome, was just a dream come true. In many ways he was the dream I never knew I had. He was supportive of me and my career, he was kind and generous, he was fun and adventurous, he became my best friend and I believed in soul mates again. You know Daph, I am divorced too. I got married when I was really young and it didn't work out so I was pretty jaded too. But I remember the first time I met you kids, I instantly fell in love with you all because you were the children, of the man I loved. I couldn't even believe how easy it was for me to love you. And Daphne, I do love you. Through all of it your mom…I can't say anything bad about your mom Daphne because I can't imagine what it would be like to have to suddenly become a single mom to three children and I know it was hard on her, but it's not because we didn't try to be there for all of you. She wouldn't have it. Then our wedding and she refused to let you kids come. Remember I asked you to be in the wedding? It broke my heart that you weren't in my wedding. But then I got pregnant, I was able to love a piece of your dad that was mine because Helen wouldn't let you see us. Your dad gave me the most precious gift I could ever have asked for. His love and my beautiful little girl. Sometimes I wake up in the morning and can hardly believe my life. I pray for your mom, I really do because we could all be so much happier if she'd quit living this lie. That's what she's living. She's hanging on to bitterness and anger over something that isn't even true. They were unhappy and couldn't live together. It wasn't anyone's fault because they were happy once upon a time, and very much in love. Your dad still loves your mom very much. He wants nothing but happiness for her."

Daphne was sobbing. "How could I go back to her? How can I go on living in that house? In that misery? I don't want to go back."

"Daphne, just so you know, you are always welcome to come live with us if you choose. We love you very much and we'll keep your rooms available for you at all times. I think your mom needs you though. When she comes back, maybe she'll be inspired to work on her problems. Maybe you can be the one to take her for walks and get her out of the house. You can do a lot for her. We're right here, and it will never be miserable for you again. You're different now. You've been exposed to a new life and you will carry that with you."

There was another knock on the door. Eric opened it and Georgie crawled in behind him.

"Girls what's going on in here?" he handed the phone to Daphne. "It's Nicole."

Daphne didn't have to speak; Nicole was all breathless excitement on the other end as she invited Daphne to the mall with her and her brother.

"Do you need any money?" Holly asked.

"No. I still have a ton from the money you've given me times before." Daphne sighed. She felt a relief at the thought of doing something fun. It'd been an early and already intense day. She was up for the mall. She hugged Holly and smiled at Eric, and then went to join her friend.

Nicole was jumping up and down by her brother's car, "come on get in, I'll introduce you in the car."

Daphne laughed hysterically. She was even more excited that her brother was in town than she was to meet Eric. Daphne got in the back seat and Nicole made the introductions. Her brother was Robert and she could only see the back of his head, and his side profile. He only said hi to her. Nicole talked non-stop. About his semester at college, if he had a girlfriend, how'd he get the new car, who were they meeting up with at the mall? Robert laughed most the time telling her occasionally she should calm down or she'd blow a fuse.

"I don't know I just love my brother." She gushed as they walked through the parking lot towards the mall. Robert was taller than Daphne was so of course that made him tall. He had blonde hair just like Nicole and beautiful green eyes. Daphne decided he was definitely cute. Cuter than Eric? That still remained to be seen. But he was very "cool". He grinned a lot, checked things out and carried himself with ease and confidence. He dressed good, he didn't dress with baggy pants, and he didn't dress up like the metrosexuals. He wore jeans that fit, and a t-shirt that said UCLA and had their mascot, a bear, on it. She noticed he wore flip flops, like her, and that he had nice tanned feet and short, clean toenails. Looking at his feet, Daphne wondered if she may have an obsession with feet remembering she'd been quite fascinated by Eric's bare feet earlier that morning.

"There's DJ." Robert said as he pointed to an even taller guy walking towards them with a tiny girl who may as well have been his poodle, she was all hair. DJ was a baggy pants wearing kid with freckles and smiling blue eyes.

"Hey bud!" the guy DJ said, "who's the hottie?" he asked as he winked at Daphne. Daphne laughed at his silly demeanor and noticed his girlfriend roll her eyes.

"This is my friend Daphne." Nicole said happily.

"You're hot Daphne. This is my girl, Che Che." He said introducing the poodle to the girls.

Che Che was breathtaking. She was a short Mexican girl made taller by platform shoes that Daphne guessed must have been seven inches high. She had beautiful, long, curly dark hair. Daphne was trying not to stare for fear that Che Che would know she was looking for pores in her perfect, mocha complexion. Her eyebrows were artistically drawn on and if Daphne could hang a poster of her on her wall as one of the most beautiful girls she'd ever seen she would. She was dressed very fashionably in a blouse that looked very soft with a wide belt and a short skirt and tons of bangles on both her wrists. DJ towered over her; he must have been at least 7 feet tall. They looked a little odd together, and at the same time seemed to fit. Che Che had a charisma that seemed to make her bigger than what she really was.

They were walking between stores when a booming voice echoed through the otherwise quiet mall.

"Nicky G in the hizzy ya'll." They all turned around and Daphne was not surprised to see Dylan Plantini and Bill Flossom walking towards them with two girls Daphne didn't recognize. Daphne noticed that Nicole didn't look pleased, she looked embarrassed and these were kids she hung out with at school.

"Hey Dylan, Bill, what's up?" Nicole asked rather simply and Daphne noticed all the excitement she had from earlier seemed to fade.

"Nine volt is that you?" Dylan asked pointing towards Daphne, "girl you slumming? Whacha doing hangin out with her?"

"Shut up." Nicole said.

Daphne could feel the heat rush through her neck and to her cheeks as she glanced sideways at Robert.

"Nine volt? Quiete tu boca culero!" Che Che said.

"Hold up Chiquita. Taker down a notch and use your inside voice." Dylan said.

"Chiquita? Aye aye aye." Che Che said, she was angry and Daphne never saw someone so small become so fierce. Che Che reminded her of those shirts that said, Sweet to Bitch in 0 seconds.

"Why you hatin pimp?" DJ said bobbing his head in front of Dylan, mocking him while Che Che was spewing all kinds of vulgarities in Spanish.

"Hey I know Spanish, I know what you're saying." Bill said.

"What Spanish you know bendejo? Uno dos tres?" Che Che said as she tried to lunge towards the guys while DJ held her back.

The girls the guys were with giggled and Che Che shot them the nastiest look Daphne had ever seen. The look quieted the girls down as quickly as they had started giggling.

"Whatever, we're out." Dylan said as they walked away.

Daphne wouldn't have been so embarrassed if it weren't for the way she noticed Robert watching her throughout the entire confrontation.

"Listen here." Che Che said as she held Daphne's hand, "you're beautiful and when you get those braces off you'll be even more beautiful so don't listen to them."

"I don't. They've called me worse." Daphne said.

"Do you girls want an Orange Julius?" Robert asked looking at Nicole and Daphne. Nicole eagerly shook her head yes. Daphne was positive if Nicole could get away with it, she would hold her brother's hand throughout the entire mall. She acted like a five year-old girl, giddy with excitement every time her brother looked at her.

Daphne instinctively reached for her back pocket to get out some money and when Robert saw her wad of cash he waved it aside. "The drink is on me kid." He winked at her and Daphne thought she could have died right there. She couldn't fight it, Robert was gorgeous, and sexy when he winked at her. She felt herself smile easily at him and wondered if she looked as awkward as she felt.

Daphne could still hardly believe that she was not only hanging out with Nicole Gaines, but a college boy was buying her an Orange Julius. Posiadyn Fisher was her dad's brother-in-law and this summer was getting better and better by the minute.

"So where's your girlfriend anyway?" Nicole asked Robert as they walked around and Daphne felt her ears get hot as she was positive her ears grew the size of frisbees waiting to hear his answer.

"She's at home in L.A. It's not that serious Nic. She's just a girl to hang out with." Robert said.

"And make out with." DJ chided.

Daphne giggled and used the opportunity of a giggle to feel her ears and make sure they were still small and attached to her head and not flapping it against it as she walked. DJ was funny. "Hey, Nicole, let's go into Bath and Body works. Che Che come with." Daphne said as they went inside. Daphne's new obsession was scented lotions. She couldn't get enough of them and had a small collection at home. She picked up some lotion for her and some lotion for her mom.

"I want to get something special for Holly. But I don't know what." Daphne said as she looked around.

"I know. What do you get the girl who has it all? My mom has a hard time shopping for her too. Like at her birthday and Christmas." Nicole said.

Daphne thought for just a second before the idea came to her.

"I've been wanting to get her some perfume. Let's head over to Sephora." Daphne suggested.

"I know what you're up to. You just want to get some more lip gloss." Nicole teased.

Daphne couldn't deny she did need to add a new lip gloss to her collection, "Do you think your brother would take me by the yarn store too? So I could pick up some yarn."

"Yeah, I'm sure he would." Nicole said.

At the end of their day Daphne had managed to pick up gifts for her mom and Holly, picked up some new yarn and lip gloss and still could go home and look forward to hanging out with Eric. Daphne didn't think life could get any better. Her life had changed so much she could barely recognize it as her own. She used to sit home and dream of fun times and now she was having them, and all the cool happenings were indeed real. Posiadyn Fisher was a real, live person. His name was Eric and he was kind, and generous and a fantastic cook and nice! Not to mention totally hot. He had walked off her walls and into her life. She had a friend who was smart and funny and totally cute. She was getting along with her step-mother and she liked it. She liked her dad again, she had a cute little sister and she was getting along with her brothers. This dream summer was more than she could ever imagine. What was better still than all of that? Daphne was changing. She was losing weight, 25 pounds so far! 25 pounds and she didn't even realize she had that much to lose. Her face was clearing up, and she could finally see the Daphne she always knew she could be.

She was excited to see her mom. Excited to share her new self yet she knew that her mom may not accept the new Daphne because she was transforming into a new person with the help of someone her mom desperately despised. Daphne hoped that when her mother returned, that she would be able to help her see that Holly wasn't a bad person.

So many thoughts went in and out of her mind that she couldn't control them, they were making her head hurt. She sat quietly in the back seat as they drove home. There were kids milling all around the house, like a block party and when they got out of the car, the whole band Aquarium had gathered together for an impromptu jam session in the garage. It was the concert Daphne hoped to one day attend and now it was in her own dad's garage and they had been waiting for her to get there before they would begin. Daphne almost died when she heard the guitar start the opening chords of her favorite song, "Along the Sea", she screamed and starting singing the words as loud as she could. Daphne and Nicole were dancing and singing along with the lyrics. Even Robert and DJ hung around to watch them play. It was warm and everywhere Daphne looked she could see smiling faces and dancing bodies. Georgie bounced her butt up and down and the twins would bang their head and run around the crowds. Daphne was impressed with her own ear and how being this close to the band she could actually hear the difference between the electric guitar and the bass guitar because when they changed their song, "Someday" from the rock version to a slow ballad played only with the electric guitar, she thought it sounded better than ever.

Daphne wanted to listen to them play all night but she was surprised at how exhausted she felt. She went in early, much earlier than most everyone, including Nicole. She couldn't get over the fact that she used to stare at her bobblehead Posiadyn and dream of the possibility that they'd come to town and she'd win tickets to see them. As she stared at the ceiling before she dozed off she could still hear Tom, also known as King Crab, playing a few strings of his electric guitar. The moonlight in the room cast a glow on her mural and it seemed as if the mural had come to life and was playing music to help her fall asleep. She could hear the laughter of Holly and Eric, her dad and the muffled voices as she drifted off to sleep and remembered it was all totally real.

6

A few days after "Posiadyn Fisher" had arrived at the house, the paparazzi had found out he was in the neighborhood and had started to camp out in front of the house. They would follow Holly and Daphne on foot while they walked around the block in the early evenings. Daphne didn't mind at all, she found it ironic that they were being followed when the real celebrity was in the house. But she loved "hiding" behind the big sunglasses that were so popular and baseball caps and either giving them a blank look or a huge smile. She even felt like a celebrity herself and reveled in the attention. The photographers weren't mean, just nosy and bothersome, but she understood their interest knowing full well that she was an avid tabloid reader. Who was she to be angry when they used to be the source she got all her information about Posiadyn Fisher from? She wouldn't have had the hundreds of pictures and posters of the band if it wasn't for those photographers.

It was all fun and games until she received a phone call from her mom in Spain.

The family was sitting around eating a Mexican feast that Eric had prepared. He'd made flautas, he'd actually mashed the beans himself, and she watched him do it! They ate ceviche and he made a soup called pasole. All while the adults drank margaritas and Daphne was so curious as to what they tasted like because she thought the drink looked cool with the big salt around the rim of the glass and the little umbrellas in the margarita slush that everyone thought was so delicious.

Daphne ran to the phone when it rang, expecting it to be Nicole. Full of excitement she squeaked out a hello before all happiness drained from her being as her mom went off on her tirade.

"Daphne do you know that your face is splattered all over Spain's issue of People magazine! This magazine is referring to you as Posiadyn Fisher's new underage girlfriend and calling you the next Priscilla Presley."

Daphne wanted to burst out laughing, but the tone in her mom's voice told her she better not breathe.

"Anyway mom, you have to know that's crazy I mean come on." Daphne was trying desperately not to giggle.

"Put your father on right now!" Helen demanded.

Daphne didn't say anything as she walked into the kitchen with the phone handing it over to her dad.

Over her dad's conversation, Daphne was trying to whisper to everyone what the freak out was about, but her dad was getting increasingly angry and her mom was hollering so loudly that he was holding the phone away from his ear and they could all hear what they were saying.

"I don't give a shit Todd, do you realize if our child is on the cover of international magazines that she could very easily be a target of greedy kidnappers! I don't want my daughter to be the next Lindberg baby. Now I'm in Spain and I can't do anything about this right now but I demand you take her to my mother's house right now!" The look of amusement and shock on her dad's face caused Daphne to finally lose it and laugh out loud. Eric and Holly didn't find it as amusing.

"First of all Helen, our daughter is in no danger. She is not having an affair with Holly's brother. Daphne is having the time of her life and I will not take her to her grandmother's house. If you're going to panic, and think you can do a better job of protecting her from harm than I can, then I would suggest you fly over here immediately and we will discuss it in court. Otherwise, I'm sorry that photos are popping up of our child, I'll make sure to ask Eric to talk to his management team and see if there is anything we can do to rectify the situation. Otherwise, have a wonderful rest of your vacation, we'll see you in a couple weeks." And he hung up on her. Her dad hung up on her mom and Daphne just looked at the phone with her mouth to the floor waiting for it to ring immediately and it didn't. In fact everyone expected her to call back and no one said anything while they waited.

"So, what's going on?" Eric finally quipped.

"Helen is flipping out. She saw a magazine calling Daphne the next Priscilla Presley and she's just stirring up trouble. She has to know it's nothing. You know I've about had it with her, we finally get the kids, finally, and it's trouble all the way, I think I should call my attorney in the morning." She'd never seen her dad so angry and seeing the red creep up his neck kind of worried Daphne.

"Todd, call him, but let's talk this out. Don't let her get the best of you."

"You know we can get them Holly. You know they'd grant us custody in a heartbeat." He said.

Daphne didn't know what he was talking about, but her heart swelled with pride at the thought that he might want them full time.

"Let's talk about it tonight ok?" Holly said, shooting him a warning look.

"I'll call my manager right now Todd." Eric got up and walked out of the room.

"Daddy could we stay here with you?" Ritchie asked.

"Maybe kiddo. We'll see." Todd said trying to remain calm but his furrowed brow let Daphne know he was up to something.

Daphne sat in silence for a moment looking between her dad and Holly and found herself clearing her plate away and headed for her room. She rather sit and knit in her room instead of visiting with the family. A custody battle wasn't something she actually wanted to go through. She was worried she'd have to testify, would she have to say mean things about her mom. Was it almost like being taken away? Did she really want to not live with her mom? As deeply in love as she was with her new summer life, she was prepared to let it go at the end of summer, did she really want it all year round? Yeah, she did want it she sighed. But at what cost? The cost of her mom living alone? Daphne knew living alone without the kids just might not be something her mom could handle. She was already depressed most the time and couldn't spend a lot of time with them when she'd get home from work. But she would often say at least she had something to come home to as she kissed them on the cheek and went into her room.

The scarf she was knitting for Eric was coming along nicely. She'd be done with it in a day or two and then she was eager to start something for Nicole's birthday. It'd never taken so long for her to complete something, but she also never had so much going on either.

Her thoughts wandered from custody battles to Nicole's golden birthday. She'd be turning 15 on August 15th. Daphne wanted to make her something really special. She'd already picked up some yarn to make her friend a pair of warm, fluffy socks for the winter. But she really wanted to make her a fuzzy pillow. Something pretty and girlie to lay her head on at night to keep all her dreams safe.

Nicole had recently confided in Daphne that she was trying to win this contest at Seventeen magazine. They were looking for super hip girls that were "in the know" about fashion, music, style and boys and Nicole thought she'd be perfect for it. So did Daphne. Although Daphne was afraid it'd mean Nicole would have to move away now that they were finally friends, Daphne wanted to keep her fears to herself lest she'd appear selfish. Nicole was talented. She was a wonderful poet and Daphne was always shocked at the wisdom and observations Nicole would write about. Nicole had also recently started writing stories and was thinking she might want to study journalism and be in the high school newspaper. She was rolling around an idea about an article she wanted to submit to Seventeen magazine, "My Summer with Posiadyn Fisher by Nicole Gaines". Everyone was convinced it'd be an easy sell, and he'd already given the okay for her to do it. Thinking back to the popular, fashionable mean person she used to know her as, Daphne was surprised to learn the true passionate soul her friend possessed. They were creative kindred spirits and Daphne wanted only the best for her friend.

As if by osmosis, Holly walked in with the phone and Nicole was on the other line. Happy to get back into her gossipy, girl world Daphne chatted with Nicole until the wee hours of the night when they decided they'd meet up at Nicole's house for breakfast.

Surprised that she would be willing to leave Posiadyn Fisher for a morning, Daphne was also surprised at how excited she was to see Nicole's brother. Not that she'd ever tell anyone, ever, he seemed to be more real to her than Eric. Nothing could ever happen between her and Eric, not that she even wished for that anymore, but there was something about a college boy that made her do her hair and makeup and try to look extra cute.

When she arrived she had hoped she didn't look so obvious since Nicole and Robert were sitting at their table in their pajamas.

"Did we say we were going anywhere?" Nicole asked wearily as she looked over Daphne.

"Well, I thought I'd be ready just in case." Daphne tried to cover as she sat down and poured herself a bowl of cereal. Nicole had a bowl, glass of juice and spoon ready for her when she arrived.

They were quiet until Robert finally spoke up.

"So what's going on with the rock star?" he asked, his eyebrow cocked looking Daphne straight in the eye and she somehow felt he was challenging her. His hair was tassled, but his green eyes were sparkling and alert and she thought she could get used to the tired look boys had in the morning.

She wished she knew something clever to say and she didn't.

"Well, there was some drama last night..." she started.

"OOOHHHH, do tell." Nicole ordered as she scooted her chair closer to Daphne's. Nicole always made her laugh, but especially when they gossiped. Nicole would always move closer to Daphne as if she could hear the gossip better if she was closer.

"Apparently, they have pictures of me in some tabloid in Spain, calling me Posiadyn Fisher's under age lover and my mom was completely outraged." Daphne explained as Nicole laughed out loud.

Daphne was surprised to see the intense interest Robert seemed to take in the story. He even stopped eating.

"What? They have pictures of you?" Robert asked.

"Of course they do. Haven't you noticed the paparazzi everywhere? They probably have pics of you, I'm surprised they haven't labeled you his gay lover." Nicole giggled, Robert rolled his eyes.

"I don't blame your mother for being pissed." He said simply and resumed eating his cereal.

Nicole and Daphne looked at each other and then looked at Robert.

"Are you kidding?" Nicole asked.

"It's not like it's true." Daphne added.

"Robert, it's lies. Her mom shouldn't have flipped out." Nicole continued.

"And she's freaking thinking I'm going to get kidnapped. She called me the Lindberg baby, I mean what is that?" she asked turning to Nicole because she knew everything but Nicole shrugged her shoulders.

Robert laughed. "I mean for all you know Daphne, he could be setting you up for publicity purposes. Any publicity is good publicity, the more salacious the better."

"Hold up, the more what? Get off the college podium and speak to us like high school ok." Nicole said shaking her head.

"I mean you sound ridiculous. Just like my mom." Daphne said, in total shock that her college crush could sound even more ridiculous than her mother. She couldn't even eat, she could only look at him with utter confusion and disgust. "She even threatened to come home early, she told my dad to take me to my grandma's house."

"I mean I don't understand your obsession with this guy anyway. He just sings songs." Robert said as he got up to put his bowl in the dishwasher.

"Um, excuse me... He cooks." Daphne said matter-of-factly.

Robert looked at her, chuckled and rolled his eyes. Daphne thought he would take off to his room or something, but he sat back down.

"Why are you hatin on Posiadyn Fisher? I thought you liked his music. I mean are you jealous? If so maybe you should take up an instrument instead of becoming an ambulance chaser." Nicole said as she shoved toast in her mouth. "Gosh, I didn't make you toast Daph! Hold on." She got up to take out the toaster.

"So that's what you're going to school for? To be an ambulance chaser? Are you going to save people?" Daphne asked innocently surprised that she was still talking to the college boy.

"What?" Robert asked.

Nicole laughed, "Daphne, an ambulance chaser is what they call lawyers who are always waiting for accidents so they can sue people for lots of money! It's supposed to be facetious. Are you thinking of an EMT? The person who drives in an ambulance."

Daphne was so embarrassed she couldn't help but laugh out loud. Even Robert started laughing.

"God you can be such a ditz." Nicole laughed.

"Is that what you thought?" Robert asked.

Daphne could only shake her head in agreement.

"You two are crazy." He said as he stood up and walked out.

"Where you going?" Nicole pouted.

"Shower" he said, his voice trailing off down the hall.

"Toast." Nicole handed it to Daphne and watched her finish her cereal.

"What do you want to do today?" Daphne asked.

"We can just hang out. Wanna meet back at your house. I need to shower. I wasn't expecting you to come all done up and stuff." Nicole said eyeing Daphne's wardrobe.

"I mean, I was kind of embarrassed, I didn't want to be all morning breath, eye boogies and jammies with your brother and stuff." Daphne said.

"He wouldn't have cared. You do look cute though. You've

lost a lot of weight. I bet we can share clothes now." Nicole said trying to pull down the back of Daphne's shirt to see the label.

"Not quite. That's probably another 50 pounds."

"Whatev." Nicole said as she stood up, "Ok honey, help yourself out, I need a shower. I'll stop by when I'm done."

Daphne felt a little awkward sitting at the table with no one with her. She didn't even finish the milk at the bottom of the bowl which was her favorite. She just dumped out the milk in the sink and put her bowl in the dishwasher.

She was heading out the door when she heard Robert's voice behind her. She thought she heard him mumble something, he laughed and she watched him collapse on the couch in the living room. She was too embarrassed to ask him if he was talking to her so instead she just smiled and waved and headed back home. She was barely out the door when she heard her name called and turned happily around to find Robert standing in the doorway.

"Daph, tonight you know, we're all going to get together at the mall. DJ and Che Che will be there, we were going to check out the new restaurant Freezeway, you're coming with Nicole right?" he asked with a grin on his face.

"Oh sure, she hadn't mentioned it, but it sounds great." She didn't know what to say. A part of her wondered if he was asking her to be there and another part wondered if he was only curious so he'd have enough money for them all. "I'll bring money, how much should I bring?"

He rolled his eyes, "you don't need to bring money."

"Oh, okay." She giggled and started to walk away feeling a massive urge to run away.

"Stay out of trouble Lolita." He said and she fought the urge to turn around and kept walking towards the house. Daphne thought it was fun that her best friend only lived a few feet away. Everyone was constantly coming and going from each other's house. Eating lunch or breakfast together, the barbecues, sharing recipes and stories and always hanging out in each other's yards. Daphne would definitely be sad when the summer was over. And what just happened with Robert? She felt like she was going to burst if she didn't talk to someone about it soon.

When Daphne got back to the house, Eric was waiting for her in the living room.

"Hey Daphne, come sit with me." Eric asked.

She sat down next to him and smiled.

"So, I'll be going down to L.A. for a few days, to shoot that video, would you be up to go with me?" he had the biggest smile on his face and she jumped off the couch.

"Are you kidding me? It's really going to happen? You really want me in the video?" she was barely able to control herself.

Eric laughed and nodded.

"ohmygodohmygodohmygod! Yes! I want to go." She shouted.

"Well, I'll have a couple of assistants and my manager will be there so you'll have plenty of people surrounding you if your mother should mention anything. We'll go up for a couple days and I thought when the shoot was over we'd go to Disneyland…"

Daphne cut him off, "Disneyland? Are you kidding me?" her eyes teared up. She was embarrassed that she seemed to be crying all the time, "I've never been to Disneyland. We've always wanted to go."

"Perfect. I figured when the shoot was finished I'd fly out everyone and we'd check it out."

Daphne nodded her head in agreement. She knew she was going to have the time of her life. Holly walked in and Daphne practically jumped in her arms.

"OH MY GOD!!! Holly, we need to talk." Daphne rushed

over to her and took the groceries from her hands as Eric started putting them away.

"What is it?" Holly asked, confused as to if Daphne was happy or upset.

"Besides the fact that I absolutely love your brother and he's taking me to LA?"

"You did it huh Eric?" Holly asked and Eric nodded and smiled as he leaned easily against the counter.

Daphne shot Eric a glance and whispered, "It's a secret Holly, we need to talk in private."

"Oh hey, I'll scoot, I've got calls to make." Eric offered as he headed out the door.

"OH MY GOD!" Daphne cried aloud when he was out of the room, "Something just happened and I don't know what it was but I swear to god if I don't spill I'll just burst."

"What is it, Daphne, you're cracking me up." Holly sat down at the table.

"Ok, I think Robert just invited me somewhere, I mean he did invite me somewhere, but I don't know if he invited me somewhere, or if he was just inviting me somewhere."

"Oh my. I don't really understand teenager anymore Daphne. I try to be cool because I've got the brother the rock star, but I'm really not cool. Why don't you try to explain it to me so I can understand?"

"Oh my god." Daphne took a breath. "uh, so I was walking out of the house and Robert said to me, 'we're going to the mall tonight to check out this new restaurant, you're coming with Nicole right?' And so I was all, 'yeah, how much money should I bring?' and he's all, 'I've got it.' Oh my god, what does that mean?"

Daphne watched a slow smile creep across Holly's face, "Well, I think it means he wants to make sure you feel welcome to come.

I would guess he wouldn't mind if you were there. But again, I'm very far removed from teenager, and I can't be quite sure. But what I am quite certain of, you should look your very best."

7

"Holly, I need your help with this. I know I have to look pretty spectacular, I want to look beautiful, but what do I have?" she dragged Holly down towards her room, Georgie toddling after them.

"Well, let's see." Holly started going through the outfits hanging in Daphne's closet. "You know, you look really good in red. It's your color, it makes your face sparkle."

"Really? My face sparkles?" Daphne stood still and looked hopefully at Holly. Her innocence and insecurity made Holly stop what she was doing. She walked over to Daphne and cupped her face in her hands.

"Oh Daphne. You're a beautiful girl, haven't you seen it? You're beautiful. You look just like your dad and maybe I'm biased, but come here." She brought Daphne to the mirror that hung over her dresser. "Look at your sparkling eyes, look at how wide and curious they are. You're gorgeous. And you have a beautiful smile, and a great personality. You look good in red, it's your color. Stop crying." Holly laughed.

"I know, I cry a lot. I can't stop." Daphne said as she watched Holly do the work.

"What about this. This is a pretty top, and I know how you love your jeans." Holly handed Daphne outfits and bent down to look at her shoes. "But you could definitely use some shoes. None of these would work. A cute pair of heels, or strappy sandals." She suggested.

"Uh no. Ew, I like flip flops. What about these?" she pointed to a pair of white flip flops. "Maybe I could glue a fake flower to them or something. I usually do crystals you know, but flowers would be a good change. With the red and all, it reminds me of flowers."

"Ok."

"But then again, maybe not. Maybe strappy sandals would be good, Robert is a college kid you know. Should I try to act older?"

"No Daphne, definitely do not act older, you are only 14. Robert is a good kid, but he is older than you and in college, in another state. Go out and have fun, but definitely don't get sprung."

"Sprung? I thought you didn't know teenager."

"Sprung isn't teenager Daphne, it's universal."

They shared a laugh and Holly kissed Daphne on the cheek. She thought it was the most tender thing anyone had ever done. She collapsed on her bed but as soon as her eyes focused on the ceiling above her, the door opened and Nicole bounded in.

"You are not asleep. Tell me you're not asleep." She said plopping down next to her.

"I'm not asleep. I'm just relaxing." She sat up.

"So I thought it'd be fun to go see a movie. We can go do that, and when we get back my brother wants to take us to dinner."

"I know. Sounds so fun."

"What do you mean you know?" Nicole asked curiously, "he just invited me."

"What do you mean?"

"Are you saying my brother already told you?" Nicole was giggling.

"Yeah, when I left a little while ago. I don't get it. What's so funny?"

"Oh my gosh Daphne. Sometimes you're kind of clueless, but it's okay. I'll try not to tell Eric, I wouldn't want him to get jealous."

"What are you talking about Nicole?"

"Oh, just the fact that you're trading in Posiadyn Fisher for my brother."

'No way!" Daphne shrieked, "Posiadyn will always and forever be my first, only and truest love. Besides your brother is a real boy, he probably has cooties."

They burst out into laughter.

"Let's go."

They headed out the door. They took the bus into town. Daphne didn't mind taking the bus because she liked to look at what people were wearing when they were downtown at the bus depot. Nicole hated riding the bus; she hated to be seen on public transportation. As Nicole chatted non stop about starting high school and her brother, Daphne wasn't paying attention. Nor did she notice all the people walking past her who pointed and whispered. She only had Robert on her mind and what she would say, and how she would say it in a restaurant with him later that night. Her thoughts were racing, like an airport with it's arrivals and departures, every thought that was figured out would be followed by a new one. It was non stop and giving her a headache. By the time they reached the theater and Nicole bought herself a large popcorn with extra butter layered in between and a large soda and bon bons, Daphne only had a quick moment to think where does she put all that food before she started wondering again if the restaurant would be dark and romantic, or be bright and casual. What if there were other girls there and what if she became really jealous? What if they had a pretty waitress and he talked to her and didn't say two words to Daphne? What if, she ordered something and when she took a bite it slopped onto her shirt? Or she ate something that got caught in her braces. And what if, Robert only invited her to be nice? It was all too much!

"Nicole, I feel sick. I just can't go tonight." She said, right in the middle of the movie, so loud that the people sitting in front of them turned to her and hushed her.

Nicole choked a little and spit the popcorn out barely missing the head of the husher guy who sat in front of them. "You're kidding right Daph? It's going to be so fun!"

"For real. I think I need to throw up. I'll be right back." She rushed down the steps and out into the lobby. She noticed that there was no one in the lobby, and the bareness of it helped her relax for a moment. She dug into her jeans and pulled out two quarters and looked for a payphone. She took a deep breath and for the first time in her recollection, she called the one person she knew she needed the most.

"Dad. I need you to take me to ice cream tonight. I'm scared and confused about something and you said if I ever wanted to do something just you and me that we could do it." Her words came falling out of her mouth so quickly that she prayed he got it all and she wouldn't have to repeat it.

"Ok hon. I'll probably be home about six, we can go after dinner, just the two of us. Is everything all right?" his voice was deep on the phone and it made her feel secure.

"Yeah dad, everything is fine. We'll talk later." She hung up the phone and went to the bathroom. She sat in the stall for a couple minutes and when she opened the stall door Nicole stood in front of her tapping her foot.

"I didn't hear any throw up. Did you throw up?" Nicole asked.

"No, I didn't but I feel like I want to. I called my dad because I just didn't feel good. He thinks I really should stay home tonight." Daphne couldn't believe she was trying to get out of doing something with Nicole, that hadn't happened. But the pressure of sitting across from Robert was too much for her to deal with. She didn't feel ready to deal with boy attention or girl competition.

Nicole sighed deeply. "It's fine. You know I just want you to come. I just want to be with my favorite people. But it's okay, we'll do something else another time." Nicole looped her arm through Daphne's and they headed for the bus stop.

Daphne was in contemplation the whole day. Her thoughts had quieted down and she enjoyed the silence in her mind, and not worrying about anything other than what she wanted from the ice cream shoppe her dad took her to.

Pick UR Ice was a neighborhood creamery that Todd explained was one of his favorite places to go for ice cream. When they walked in Daphne liked it immediately because she loved watching the girls who worked behind the counter blend the ice cream together. Blending your own ice cream was something she never could have imagined you could do, but there she stood watching people pick chocolate ice cream with strawberries, or coffee flavored ice cream with oreo cookies.

"Dad, this is like déjà vu. I feel like I've been here before." Daphne stood in line looking at the people around her. Sitting in the corner at a small table was a woman with short blonde hair and glasses, she was pretty and smiling at a guy whose back was to Daphne. At the register was a short man, wearing a baseball cap and a bright orange shirt and holding a little blonde haired girl who looked back at her. Behind her was a beautiful dark haired woman who smiled back at her, she was holding hands with a little brown haired girl who smiled at her too. The two behind her were identical and it didn't take much to know they were mother and daughter. Daphne noticed the huge diamond earrings the woman was wearing, they were the biggest earrings she'd ever seen and was positive they must be real. She was so wrapped up in looking at everyone she didn't realize it was her turn.

"Daph," her dad nudged.

"Oh yeah. Um, can I have the vanilla bean with the wafers and drizzle some chocolate in there." She was really excited to watch how they'd fold it all together.

"Drizzle some chocolate?" Todd laughed.

"I know, I know, sometimes the strangest things come out of my mouth, it's like someone is putting words in my mouth, but I have no idea who." Daphne shrugged.

There was something about the couple in the corner that Daphne was particularly drawn too and threw her napkin away as an excuse to get a glimpse of the guy that she couldn't see. He looked up at her and winked, she noticed he had green eyes and smiled at her with a smile so dazzling it was like watching the sun come out. His smile completely transformed his face. She felt her heartbeat stop for the briefest second and followed her dad out the door. She felt a little dizzy the way everyone was so friendly and familiar and she almost ran over another couple that was coming in as she was walking out. She looked directly into the light blue eyes of a beautiful blonde who smiled at Daphne with one of the most beautiful smiles she's ever seen. The man she was with held the door open for Daphne and she noticed that he had strong arms and looked like Orlando Bloom.

Once Daphne was outside she looked back once more.

"Well that was sort of weird dad, did you notice all the people in there?"

"No. So do you want to eat our ice cream here?" he pulled out a chair for the small white plastic tables that were outside the creamery and she sat down.

She was lost in her own world for a couple minutes, still trying to figure out where she knew all those people from. Maybe a dream or something, she thought to herself before she decided that she had no idea what had just happened.

"Well dad, thanks a lot for bringing me here. I definitely needed a sec from the hectic that is your house."

"Yeah, it has been a little crazy, but you're having fun right kiddo?" he looked at her and she could tell he desperately wanted her to say yes.

"I'm having so much fun dad that I don't know how I could ever go back to mom's. It's so hard there, she's so hard to live with." She sighed wondering if she should have said it to her dad.

"You're telling me. It was pretty rough for me too for awhile there." She liked the way her dad paid attention to what she was saying, he looked her straight in the eye like she was the most interesting person he'd ever talked to.

"Can you tell me anything good about mom? I don't remember anything good about her. Just drama." She asked and put her ice cream aside.

"Well, your mom..." it took him a moment and then he smiled, "once upon a time, your mom was my best friend."

"Yeah?" she asked and noticed he looked wistful.

"You know we met in college. She was beautiful of course and we had a class together. One class and I don't remember which one but we had a group project to do and she and I were the only ones that actually worked on it. We had to exchange numbers and we'd complain to each other about being the only ones who were working on it. She made me laugh, she was very funny, clever and smart and we started hanging out a lot. We dated and traveled and I knew I wanted to grow old with her. At the time I met your mom, I'd never felt love before, so I thought she was the one. We moved in together, we got married and she started teaching while I finished up my degree. She wanted kids right away and I really wanted to wait for a while, it was important to me back then to be settled, I wanted to do it right and make sure my family didn't want for anything. I think she harbored a little resentment about that because after we'd had you she would sometimes throw it in my face how she supported us. After the twins came, we were overwhelmed and by that point we'd outgrown each other. We just didn't seem to have anything in common anymore, we couldn't talk about anything without fighting. We just drifted apart. I still love her very much. I know who she is and who she can be."

"Do you think you'll get back together?" Daphne asked, a little frightened. She couldn't imagine her dad with anyone other than Holly.

"Oh no, no no no no no. No Daph. I'm in love with Holly. I have the real thing now. You're mom and I, we aren't very compatible. I wanted to grow old with your mom but I couldn't, I can grow old with Holly. Holly is fun, and light, and young at heart, growing old with Holly wouldn't be like growing old at all, but your mom, she's very grown up, very business like about everything. We were both too grown up about our life and who was in control and a couple needs to balance each other. They need to be themselves and still be part of a couple and we could never find that groove. But I do miss her. I do miss my friend."

Daphne looked at her dad and felt sad. She felt sad that her parents were two pretty great people who couldn't work it out. She was sad that she'd missed those years that her mom had kept them all apart, and she felt sad for her own future and what relationships would mean to her then. She was glad that she didn't go out with her friends and that she was able to spend some time with her dad and she was glad that she was only 14, and all that she really had to worry about was school and clothes and having fun.

"Come on dad, let's go home. There's a rock star I want to hang out with." He smiled at her and nodded and as he got up, she did something she was sure she must have done as a toddler but couldn't remember; she held his hand.

8

Nicole made it a point to try to make Daphne feel bad for not going to dinner by telling her for days how good the food was and how much they laughed all night, but Daphne had no time to pay attention. Daphne was too busy shopping for new luggage and some new outfits for the evenings for her vacation to LA. Daphne didn't know the first thing about picking out luggage except that she wanted hers to be pink. Apparently luggage is a huge deal to those who travel a lot.

Daphne was also surprised to try on clothes. She had started the summer out a size 13 and was down to a 5. A total of 40 pounds she'd lost. She couldn't believe it. Daphne didn't look like the same person, she didn't feel like the same person, yet she was. She knew she still had dreams and hopes and fears, only now in a smaller body with a clear complexion and an overall happier life. The biggest surprise about their shopping trip was that for the first time that she could remember, she tried on bathing suits. That was the biggest triumph of all. She was excited to buy a couple really pretty dresses, she was a jeans girl, but the dresses were so pretty that she found herself wanting to buy a sewing machine and make some for herself. She could see herself in polka dot halter dresses, circa the 50's with flippy hair and gloves. As Daphne sat in her bed the night before her flight, the moonlight shining between her curtains she looked at the bags in front of her bedroom door and made a mental list of what they contained. She actually had a carryon for her makeup and toiletries like shampoo and conditioner, lotions and perfume and couldn't believe she had so much of that stuff that she needed a separate bag. She had a tote bag that held her knitting supplies and something to remind of her Nicole: an issue of Seventeen magazine. Daphne never read it, always opting to buy Popstar magazine so she could tear out the posters of Posiadyn. She didn't need to buy them anymore since she had real pictures of him, many of them with her in them.

In a few hours, she'd be on a plane, headed to LA. Home of Hollywood, beaches and Disneyland. A place where dreamers went to make their mark on the world. She wondered if she'd be "discovered" while she was there. She snorted at the thought, discovered for what she wasn't sure, but it was fun to imagine. She pinched herself to make sure it was all real. She didn't know what to expect and wondered if there were any celebrities she would see. She wondered if she'd make more celebrity friends.

Daphne thought of her mom. She hadn't told her she was going. Daphne was afraid her mom would somehow take her excitement and turn it into something terrible. The trip Daphne would keep to herself. She could tell her mom about it later. And for the first time that summer, Daphne felt no guilt over doing something she and her mother could only dream about. She had finally realized that her mom wasn't a dreamer like her, and maybe her mom didn't mean to be such a prevential person, but she was, and Daphne wouldn't let it hold her back any more.

When they boarded the plane she was excitedly prepared to sit in first class, but Eric explained that the most interesting people sat in coach. All she did was say, oh well, and he upgraded their tickets. She was impressed because she didn't think she sounded disappointed, but he seemed to pick up that this was her first flight, and it should be different and special. The flight turned out to be more fun than what Daphne thought it would be. She loved being in the air and watching the earth pass below her. She couldn't get over the fact that they were flying above the clouds and thought it was amazing, this flying machine taking her to the world of fantasy and make believe. Daphne absolutely loved first class, she loved the cushioned seats, and she loved the pampering she received from the flight attendants. Daphne liked the feeling of being special. They were able to exit the flight first, which allowed her to touch her feet in Los Angeles even sooner.

When they got off the plane they were met by Eric's management team, and the paparazzi. Daphne was getting used to the photographers by now, so she just looked straight ahead as they were led through LAX to a limousine that waited for them outside.

Once inside the limo she was finally introduced to Eric's team.

Tom Hollister was Eric's manager. He looked close to Eric's age with curly hair and sunglasses. He wore a business suit and rattled off what time they had to be on the set the next morning. He wasn't friendly at all and spent most of the time talking on the phone. There was Tiffany who sat very close to Eric and Daphne intuitively became very jealous and wondered if they were a thing. She was his assistant and looked very young. She was average looking with mousy brown hair and almond shaped brown eyes. Daphne noted that she wore very little makeup. Daphne really thought everyone in Los Angeles was beautiful, and this Tiffany defied that belief. She wasn't that nice to Daphne either, but she at least acknowledged her presence. Carol Louise was his agent, she like Tom barely noticed Daphne and was also on a cell phone the whole time. Carol was older, but very sophisticated, dressed all in black with her dark hair pulled in a bun. She wore big sunglasses but Daphne could tell she wore a ton of makeup. Her foundation was caked on and her lipstick was very dark. She had a huge bag like the one Daphne saw all the famous girls in the tabloids hold. In real life she thought it was just ugly. She thought to herself she could probably make a bag herself and made sure to make a mental note to add handbag designer to her list of things she wanted to be.

Daphne sat quietly as she listened and watched them all interact.

They arrived at the Château Marmont Hotel. It looked very old and fancy.

"We're not staying at his house." Daphne asked Tiffany.

"No one in LA ever stays at their own home Daphne." Tiffany said matter-of-factly.

"I don't live here Daphne, I live in New York. L.A. sucks." Eric said and he winked at her.

Daphne watched as these people who barely looked at her took all her bags as she followed Eric straight up to the room.

It was a huge suite with four rooms and a view of the pool. Daphne fell in love with her surroundings, they were very luxurious and she felt a sense of history and excitement as she looked around trying to absorb everything and not look like some average kid. She was intimidated by these people.

"Ok, it all sounds great, did you get the reservations?" Eric looked to Tiffany.

"Yeah, they're ready when you are." She said as she smiled sweetly at Eric.

Daphne definitely didn't like this Tiffany person. She didn't like that she wasn't very nice to her, but was giving Eric that eye.

That didn't seem like a good person. And shouldn't Eric like someone more cute?

"Ok Daph. We're going for the Hollywood star treatment now. We're going to the Ivy." Eric smiled wide. "Do you want to change or anything?"

"I don't know should I? Is it a club or something?" she asked.

"It's a restaurant where you go specifically to be seen. Just keep in mind paparazzi will be there, and your picture will end up in the papers." Carol said.

Daphne looked at what everyone else was wearing and what she was wearing: just jeans and t-shirt she redesigned. This one was a white t-shirt that had "...by daphne" stenciled on the front in hot pink and flip flops that she glued pink crystals onto. Pretty much her signature look and she felt totally comfortable with how she looked. She was hoping to look casual, hip and relaxed which she thought people in L.A. were. She went to her carryon bag and pulled out a bright orange scarf made out of bohemian yarn that she knit and wrapped it around her neck.

"Hey, I'm good to go." She smiled and stood next to Eric.

On the ride over Eric pointed out all the Hollywood landmarks on the way. There were a dozen photographers on the street opposite the restaurant and she could hear them snapping as soon as she stepped on the curb. They were calling out to Eric and asked "who's the girl" but he simply smiled and walked passed them. They were ushered right to a table out on the patio and Daphne couldn't help but look around to see if she recognized anyone, but she didn't.

The food they ordered was good, but not great and Daphne immediately knew why they didn't come for the food. She wondered why this was the place that everyone wanted to be seen at? How curious to think that one particular place would be where everyone had to go. Maybe it was because of the outside tables with the photographers across the street, or maybe it was because it was reputed to be the place to be seen. Whatever it was, Daphne was there, and she was with Posiadyn Fisher. She felt so "Hollywood" that she could feel herself leaning over the table, paying close attention to everything he was saying, thinking it made her look cool and they were in on some special secret.

After dinner Eric took her to the Griffith Park observatory to look at the stars and see the view of the city. His entourage went with them everywhere and Daphne knew for sure she didn't like a group of people around at all times. She liked the feeling of more one on one interaction. Eric was very attentive to her, and wanted her to have a good time, but Daphne wasn't used to people following her around and just being there and not saying anything. She felt like they were there to keep tabs on her and felt they were actually more bothersome than the people flashing light bulbs in her face all the time.

That first day in LA was fun and she was eager to see what the next day would be like. Eric's people had already prepped her that she would probably spend long hours in a trailer so she thought of it as an opportunity to finish the scarf she had started for Posiadyn Fisher but would give to Eric.

A couple times she was allowed on the set and would sit in the little director's chair that had Posiadyn embroidered on the back. She would have her knitting in her lap and observe the crazy director shouting all over the place. Director Lou was a short, stocky man with balding hair that had Daphne in stitches. He didn't talk like normal people; he shouted and would emphasize certain words that really meant nothing.

"In the next SHOT, you WANT the girl, but you can't HAVE her." Daphne looked down trying to stifle her giggles. She was afraid that if he caught her laughing he'd kick her out of the video. He turned to the young actress playing the lead and said, "You're

TRAUMATIZED, get it? The ROMANCE can't BE. Ok, ACTION!"

He stood there silent as the music blared throughout the studio.

"CUT! CUT! TiTi, get out HERE!" Director Lou looked like he was about to burst something. Daphne was silently beginning to worry about him.

Out of nowhere Daphne watched as the tallest, black girl she'd ever seen walk over to the director.

"Yes." She said with a very thick accent.

"Fix it! Something isn't RIGHT! They don't look HIP enough!" he said.

TiTi looked at Eric and the girl and rolled her eyes. She looked around at everyone and when she spotted Daphne she tilted her head to the side and walked straight to her.

Daphne was very intimidated by this very large girl. As she got closer Daphne thought she was quite beautiful with her very big, very dark eyes. She didn't wear a stitch of makeup and even though her skin was very dark, Daphne could see the glow and rose in her cheeks.

"You, I see you before. You here." She pointed to a picture of Daphne in a magazine TiTi had rolled in her hand. The picture had obviously been taken of her the day before when she was at the Ivy. Daphne's eyes widened at how fast the picture was published. It was the first time she'd actually seen herself in a magazine and she was embarrassed.

"Where you buy this shirt? Who your stylist. This look very hip." TiTi was even bigger the closer she stood near Daphne.

Daphne could barely catch her breath at first. "I made that shirt. I'm only 14, I don't have a stylist." She stammered.

"No stylist? No bag? Very hip. Here, what's this?" TiTi grabbed the scarf Daphne held in her lap.

"I'm knitting a scarf. It's not finished."

TiTi in a heart beat pulled Daphne's knitting needles out of the scarf causing Daphne to gasp in fear that the whole thing would become unraveled and took it to Eric where she wrapped it around his neck. She tore off the sleeves of the girl's shirt and made the actress take off her shoes. "What you think?" TiTi turned and asked Daphne.

"It looks good." Daphne didn't know what she was supposed to say. Then TiTi looked to Director Lou who looked through the camera.

"Let's TRY it again. PLACES! And ACTION!" Aquarium's music came on and she watched as the girl played with Eric and laughed and buried her face in the scarf which had now become a prop. Daphne could hardly believe that the unfinished scarf that she was knitting was in a music video. Daphne felt a flutter in the soul of her stomach that told her no matter what happened when her mom got home, her life officially would never be the same again. The feeling was so overwhelming that it shocked her a little, she'd never felt something and been so sure of anything in her life. She had seen a side of life that was fun, and exciting and extraordinary. She'd seen that sometimes, there was magic in life, and Daphne was resolved to make sure she never let herself become so unhappy ever again.

Daphne's part in the video was to be the lead's sister. In the scene Daphne was in they were supposedly at their home and in a kitchen baking a cake. The "girlfriend" was sitting on the counter top while Daphne made the cake and Eric kept taking the flour tossing it at the girl which of course would turn into a flour war. It was supposed to be young and fun. Pretending to adore Eric and have fun with her "brother" was fun, but having to get the flour out of her hair on the way back to the hotel was another thing entirely. She thought about how exciting it was to be on a "set" in Hollywood, but she was also bored with the long hours that they did nothing. She decided for sure she couldn't be an actress

Back at the hotel, the room was constantly bustling with activity. Tiffany didn't leave Eric's side although Todd and Carol left. Shell Salmon came to the room without his supermodel girlfriend which disappointed Daphne a little because she couldn't say she knew another celebrity. Fishy sat on a couch playing video games with his girlfriend who Daphne thought was rather plain. She was outgoing enough, she tried to be funny, but she had her hair in a ponytail and wore baggy jeans and a tank top which said to Daphne that she didn't have any kind of original style. Daphne sat on a chair and watched Eric talk to different music industry people and she thought it seemed very busy and complicated. She missed her dad, and Holly and Nicole. She missed the comfort of her room. She looked at Eric across the room who winked at her and held up his finger signaling to her he'd be off the phone soon. When he hung up he walked over to her.

"Are you okay? Are you tired?" he asked looking down at her.

"I am tired. How do you do it? It's so busy in here, with so many people."

"It's not like this all the time Daph. I've been hanging out with you guys and then I'll go back home to New York and have my normal life."

Daphne didn't know what to say, this life although it was fun and glamorous didn't seem normal at all. Maybe it was just the longevity of the day taking it's toll on her. She got up and kissed him on the cheek and went into her room. Daphne lay quietly in her room trying to go to sleep she thought of how much fun she'd been having with Eric. She felt like they were friends. She felt like he was someone she could trust. Daphne felt her feelings of love as an infatuated fan had turned into the warm love she had for the people in her family. It was dark in the room, and she felt content, like when she'd had a delicious dinner and left room for dessert. Daphne felt like her life was falling into place. A sting pierced her heart at the realization that it would soon be time to go back home and Eric would be leaving, Daphne felt strong enough that she could conquer anything that would come her way.

Daphne had a wakeup call the next morning at 6 am to get ready for their day at Disneyland. Groaning she picked up the phone and hung it up knowing that in less than two weeks she'd be getting used to the shrill scream of an alarm once again when she started high school.

Eric met her in the "living room" of the suite to go downstairs to the lobby.

"Good morning" he smiled, his blue eyes sparkling.

Daphne walked over to him and gave him a big hug. It was the first time she'd hugged him.

"What's this about?" he laughed and hugged her back. Daphne felt warmth in their embrace that equaled that of her dad and she felt like she could stay in his arms forever.

"Thank you Eric. Thank you for everything you've done. Thank you for coming and thank you for being Holly's brother." She sighed.

"I had fun with you all this summer. Let's go have some more!" he said and he nodded to Tiffany as they walked out of the suite.

As the doors to the elevator opened to the lobby, Daphne caught a glimpse of something she wasn't expecting and found herself running across the lobby of the Chateau Marmont.

"What! What are you guys doing here?" standing before her was Holly, her dad, the twins, Georgie and Nicole! Nicole and Daphne were hugging each other and Daphne was jumping up and down.

"He flew us out so we that we could enjoy Disneyland together!" Todd said.

"I am soo excited! I haven't been here since I was eleven." Nicole said as the group headed out to two waiting Denalis.

"This is perfect!" Daphne said as she and Nicole linked arms.

"Where are the limos?" Ritchie asked looking around.

"We're going to try to be less conspicuous at Disneyland. We don't want any unnecessary attention at the park. Then the whole experience wouldn't be as fun." Eric explained.

"I could so get used to being driven around." Nicole said on the way to the park.

"No kidding! Do you think it would save them money or cost more if instead of getting me a car on my 16th they got me a driver?" Daphne laughed.

"Would it be a car and a driver?" Nicole asked.

"You're right, there would still be a car that needs to be driven!" Daphne sighed as she watched the passing scenery.

Besides seeing all the signs that said Disneyland, Daphne knew they were at the park because Nicole was a screechy tour guide.

"Oh Daphne look, there's Space Mountain."

"Oh my gosh! Look, there's the entrance." Daphne could only laugh at her excitement.

As they piled out of the car, Daphne looked at the manicured trees and watched people of all ages and races walking to the ticket booths. They didn't have to stand in line. Eric had already bought their tickets so they went right into the park.

"Oh look there's Mickey" the twins shouted.

Daphne looked at the Mickey figure in front of the park. As everyone walked under the tunnel that led to the park, a plaque caught her attention and she stopped to read the words inscribed there.

"HERE YOU LEAVE TODAY AND ENTER THE WORLD OF YESTERDAY, TOMORROW AND FANTASY"

The words caused Daphne's eyes to tear up. As she watched Posiadyn Fisher walk into the park, with a woman named Holly who once upon a time she hated, and a girl named Nicole who once upon a time hated her, she knew that reality was a place where anything could happen. She was touched that in the most magical place on earth, made famous by wondrous fairy tales and happy memories, she knew a secret and the secret was that dreams didn't only come true in fairy tales; they came true in real life too.

Daphne was enjoying herself so much in Disneyland that she could feel the smile plastered on her face. She felt like she had officially turned into the eternally happy Holly. Everywhere she looked families were smiling and laughing and taking pictures in front of Dumbo, or the Haunted House. They'd stood in line for every ride and bought so many souvenirs that Daphne didn't know where she was going to put them all. She and Nicole bought matching sweatshirts and Daphne bought one for her mom too, hoping she'd realize Daphne couldn't stop thinking of her.

While Nicole and Daphne stood in line to buy some fries at one of the little cafes, a boy with dirty blonde hair and green eyes standing behind them in line started a conversation with them. He stood with a kid with blue eyes and white blonde hair and wore a sweatshirt that read University of Nevada Reno.

"Have you guys been on Space Mountain yet?" Nicole and Daphne looked at the boy and looked at each other.

"Not yet, is it cool?" Nicole asked.

"It's really fun. You should go on it. Are you guys from here?"

"No, we're on vacation." Nicole said as they moved forward in line. Daphne thought the green eyed boy was cute, but he was talking so easily to Nicole. "Is that where you're from? Reno?"

"Yeah, we're here on vacation too. What's your names?"

"I'm Heidi, and this is Samantha." Nicole said and Daphne tried not to laugh.

"I'm Eddie," said the green eyed boy, "this is Matt," and the white haired boy put up his hand in a wave.

They moved up in line and it was Daphne and Nicole's turn to order. As Nicole ordered their fries, Daphne thought it was time to come out of her shell. Once she started asking Eddie about what his favorite rides were, he seemed more interested in her than Nicole. While they all stood around talking, Daphne was thrilled. It was the first time she'd actually talked to a cute boy who was her age. It was another change in her life and she couldn't get over how great it felt. When it was time to get back to their families, Eddie and Daphne promised to look each other up on Myspace. She had no idea what that was, but Nicole said she'd help her.

Daphne felt in her heart, her life truly was on a different path. She was different, and couldn't even remember her old self.

9

With only one week of summer left, Daphne felt a bittersweet mix of emotions. She was sad that Eric would be leaving and she wasn't quite sure when she'd see him again. Her love for him had changed and grown. At the same time, she was excited to start high school. Her and Nicole had been planning all summer what they would join, or start and she thought it might just turn out to be fun. She found it hard to believe that only a few months earlier she wanted to drop out and be home schooled.

As the date for Daphne's mom to come home grew nearer, Holly kept her promise to go to the house and straighten out her other room.

Daphne was slightly embarrassed for them to see how disorganized her mom was. Even when it was clean, it was messy and no one living in the house for a summer caused it to smell musty and old as they walked in. The house was dark from the curtains being closed and it felt like no one lived there. Daphne could feel the lack of life in the house cause the hairs on her arms to stand up.

Daphne opened the blinds as Nicole headed to the kitchen to

find something to snack on. Georgie was tearing through the twins' video games and Holly stood quietly taking it all in.

"I can really feel your mom's unhappiness. It hangs heavy in the air." Holly said quietly.

Daphne stood next to her feeling it too. The house was night and day from where she'd just stayed for the past three months and like she'd been dreading, Daphne could feel the unhappiness start to wear down her legs and creep up into her arms.

"Let's go to your room." Holly said, scooping up Georgie as they walked into Daphne's room.

Daphne looked around the room and saw the girl she once was. Her walls covered with posters of Aquarium and Posiadyn Fisher. Her bed was still unmade and she picked up her baskets full of yarn and put them on the bed. Her TV looked small on the old, plastic TV stand that had stickers all over it. Nicole sat down to look at the old scratch and sniff sticker of Strawberry Shortcake and Lisa Frank stickers.

"Wow, some of these stickers look really old." Nicole remarked.

Daphne walked over to her closet full of old board games that she knew half the pieces were missing. A few wire hangers with clothes hanging off them instead of hanging on them. Her bobblehead of Posiadyn looked totally lifeless and once upon a time it had been her favorite little treasure.

"So what do you want to do?" Holly asked.

"Get rid of all of it. Take the posters down. Those clothes won't fit me anymore. Just my craft stuff I'll keep my scrapbooks and photo albums. Everything I want to keep I'll put on the bed." Daphne said as Nicole started taking posters off the wall.

Holly walked out of the room to get the supplies they'd need to paint the walls. A new bedroom set would be delivered later on in the day and Daphne's new comforter set would be arriving later in the week at her dad's house.

Nicole filled a large, black garbage bag full of posters and little toys that she'd taped pictures of Posiadyn Fisher to. How funny she thought that the childhood dream of knowing him and talking to all those posters would be replaced with actual photographic memories she'd shared with the real person. He was no longer Posiadyn Fisher, but her friend Eric, who she'd never lose track of.

Nicole had a bag full of all of Daphne's ugly, old clothes that were so worn and stained that as Daphne watched them leave her closet she could barely remember the time she actually wore them. She looked at her clothes in sadness realizing for the first time that she had taken no pride in her appearance to continue to wear such tattered clothes. She shook off the urge to cry, and the urge to blame her mother. In Daphne's heart she knew all she ever had to do was ask her mom to get her some new clothes. Why had she never bothered?

Daphne tossed into the trash her old tubes of lip gloss and mascara that she would wear only in her room. As more bags were filled Daphne realized she didn't have many things at all. She had no photos of her family up, no souvenirs from trips they had taken, or places they'd visited. These bags were filling up with paper junk. Posters and even trash that she hadn't realized she even had. Soda cans and Pringles cans and candy wrappers and throughout all of it Daphne was surprised that Nicole never said a word. She was embarrassed at her own sloppiness, but unsure of how exactly it had become so bad. When had she forgotten to simply throw things away?

Wouldn't someone say something? Like, holy cow, how did you live like this? They seemed to know something that Daphne was just realizing. Sometimes, things get out of control, and then something will happen, and you can come, and just straighten it all out. She couldn't believe that once upon a time these were her treasures. All she had to dream of was a poster that hung on the wall. Her dreams would now be replaced with memories.

When the room was finally bare, so was Daphne. The only thing that remained of the old Daphne was her crafting supplies. Bags full of scrap booking supplies and knitting needles. Her glue gun and crystals all in little shopping bags that lined the hallway because she didn't have drawers to put them in. Her room was empty. No posters or clothes remained. Her stereo and mirror were in the closet. They painted the walls a very light pink. Daphne wanted to be her girly self now, but not too girly. When they were done painting and needed it to dry they worked on the living room.

Daphne looked around again with the light streaming in and realized her mom had straightened it up a bit. They just really needed newer furniture. Everything just looked old and tattered and it was symbolic of how they'd been living their life; they weren't, they were only going through the motions. Daphne compared it to all the new stuff that Holly and her dad had. Although she liked to think the stuff in her mom's house had sentimental value, it just looked old. It didn't look like antiques, it just looked like old stuff that they couldn't afford to replace or simply didn't care to. The only thing Daphne knew for sure was that from here on out she would help her mom keep it organized, because now she cared, and now she wanted a life.

They organized the books on her mom's book shelf, vacuumed and lit aroma therapy candles to make it smell better. They rolled up the boys' video game cords and put them on the shelves of the entertainment center.

"Daph, whatever you do, just don't tell your mom I was the one who helped you." Holly asked.

"Holly, I'm going to tell her you were here. I am going to make sure she sees what a good person you are." Daphne said.

"She might not see it that way. I don't want to cause any grief when we're trying to make her homecoming peaceful." She said.

Holly's phone rang while Daphne continued dusting. Nicole sat on the couch "supervising" as Georgie ran in circles.

"What?" Holly asked into the phone, "Are you kidding me?" Daphne laughed at Holly's excited response that sounded so much like her own.

Holly put the phone on her shoulder.

"Daphne, it's Eric, you are not going to believe this! TiTi the stylist who worked on the video got you a deal with Fred Segal! They want to buy some of your scarves!" Holly was excited.

"Who's Fred Segal? I don't understand, I mean, I don't even have any scarves! She took an unfinished scarf and used it for that video!" Daphne said, unsure of what was happening.

Holly continued talking and murmuring a series of yeahs and okays.

Nicole looked at Daphne.

"They want to meet with you. Daphne, Fred Segal is a department store in Hollywood where celebrities and people with money shop all the time. They want to buy your scarves, this is a big deal." Holly said and sat down like she needed to breathe herself.

"But Holly, I don't have any more scarves..." Daphne couldn't finish her sentence Holly had stood up and began to pace a little.

"I've got to talk to your father. Are we done here, can we go?" Holly said as she went after the baby.

"Yeah, we can go." Daphne said, "oh, but what about the furniture? Don't we have to be here when they deliver it?"

Holly took a big sigh and sat back down. Within minutes she

was talking to her dad and making plans to meet at the house as soon as they could. It took a couple minutes for Holly to calm down so that she finally could explain to Daphne this "exciting" news.

"Daphne, the buyers at Fred Segal want to meet with you and buy your scarves. It simply means you could make some money, potentially a lot of money kiddo. This is the kind of break people dream about. Your scarves could be seen by people who set trends and your life could go in a whole new direction." Holly said.

"But couldn't they tell that scarf wasn't finished? I can't believe they'd want to buy something like that. And would I have to make like hundreds of scarves? I mean, I couldn't do that. There's no way I could do that with school and life and stuff. It sounds exciting, but doesn't sound possible."

"Well, your dad and I will go with you and we'll discuss their plan. We'll see what the order is and how we can help you make it happen. This is money you can have to pay for your college Daphne. This is money that can help you have a future."

"It sounds really cool Daph." Nicole said.

"It's weird huh?" Daphne said as she watched Nicole's big blue eyes fill with excitement.

"It's cool though." And they all sat down and looked at each other.

Daphne could barely comprehend what was happening. How an unfinished scarf could interest a department store. They all sat in silence, even while the furniture was delivered and it was time to go back to her dad's house.

When they could finally leave her mom's house and go back to her dad's house she felt despair knowing it would be Eric's last night. It hadn't hit her until the drive home. Even with the possibility of a career at the tender age of 14 to do what she daydreamed about, be a scarf designer, she couldn't shake the despair over the fact that Eric would be leaving in the morning. She'd decided she wouldn't go to the barbecue they were planning for him. She couldn't say goodbye and hoped that by pretending he wasn't leaving, then he actually wouldn't.

Eric came to her room to try to talk to her.

"Long day huh?" Eric said as he sat down on the floor next to her. "Hey, that's actually kind of a cool mural huh?"

Daphne couldn't even laugh as she looked at it.

"I don't want you leave." She said simply.

"I know, it's been a fun summer. Now it's time for me to go back to work. Need to get into the studio and work on some new songs." He said.

"Why does the summer have to be over so soon?" she asked and she rested her head on his shoulder.

Daphne started to cry and turned her body so that she could hug him. It seemed unfair to think of how long it took for her to feel comfortable around him and to think of him as a normal person, and how long it had been before she could hug him the way she'd hug anyone else in her family. It seemed like only yesterday she was this overweight, pimply teenager that just dreamed of seeing him in concert, and here he was, her friend, and he was about to leave. It was like he was going to walk into that mural and never return.

She sobbed into his shirt for a couple minutes before she calmed down.

"I could never thank you enough for all that you've done for me." She said and she looked at him. For the first time since she'd known him she looked deeply into his eyes. She saw all the kindness and love of a real person and not the still gaze of a rock star in a poster. She felt the lightness of his personality and the ease at which she could be with him. "You came here, and you became my friend, and you took me to Disneyland and Hollywood and..." she couldn't finish, the tears came again.

"Daphne, you're family. You are my family. Anytime you need anything, you call me. You know how to reach me. I'll always be here for you. I may not be with you, but I'm here for you." He told her.

"I love you. Thank you so much. Eric, thank you." She hugged him for what felt like an eternity. She didn't want to let him go, but knew she had to.

"Come on. There's a surprise downstairs." She reluctantly got up and followed him to the backyard where she noticed that everyone was milling around and there were happy birthday banners hanging in the trees.

"We're having a surprise party for Nicole. The band is over there." Eric pointed to the make shift stage built off to the side where the band was tuning their equipment.

"She's going to die!!! You're the best!" Daphne said and she kissed him on the cheek. He touched his cheek and acted like he was going to faint when she kissed it then he winked and jogged off to the stage. Daphne watched him when the crowd erupted into a chorus of "SURPRISE" and clapping and she turned around to see Nicole standing there with this huge goofy smile on her face.

The band busted out with a guitar rendition of Happy Birthday and all the kids ran over to the stage.

Daphne and Nicole sat on the grass, and Daphne gave her the socks and the pillow she made for Nicole, and also a friendship bracelet she had made.

"This is the best birthday ever. Thank you Daphne!"

Daphne looked across the yard and saw Robert heading their way. She was secretly thrilled to see him since she'd been so busy that she hadn't had much time to talk to him before he went home.

"Hey brother! Look what Daphne made for me, she's so talented." Nicole sang as he sat on the grass next to them. "Yeah I heard you got some big fashion deal or something." He grinned.

"Oh I don't know about that, but I guess it'll give me some cash for my future. That's not bad." Daphne said.

"Before you leave tomorrow, let's make Daphne a Myspace page, we met some cuties in LA that we need to look up." Nicole asked as she rocked her head back and forth to the music.

Daphne watched Robert watch the band play. She felt a little flip flop in her stomach thinking to herself how really cute he was and she didn't know when she'd see him again. She desperately wanted to say something to him, but didn't know what. She summoned all the courage she could find and asked Robert, "So if you help me with my page, will you be friends with me on Myspace?" she noticed Nicole give her a sly look and grin and continue to bob her head.

"I don't know. I'll think about it." He grinned and Nicole slapped his arm. He put his arms behind him and leaned on the grass and she looked at his profile as he stared up at the stars above. She liked the straight line of his nose and the fullness of his bottom lip and couldn't wait to start talking to him on the computer. She'd just have to get one for her home first.

Daphne giggled, she couldn't get over the reality of watching her favorite band play live. Shell came out of his shell when he wasn't in front of cameras and was just as funny as the other band members. King Crab was terribly flirtatious with all the girls and they were all cuter than she realized although Eric would always be her favorite.

Aquarium was playing in the backyard, the stars were bright in the night sky and Daphne felt more joy than she'd felt in her whole life.

Life was a dream come true.

10

The best summer of Daphne's life came to a close the day a limousine waited outside to take Eric to LA so he could work on his next album. Daphne cried all day unable to actually say goodbye because it was the hardest thing she'd ever had to do. She wasn't only saying goodbye to one of her best friends, but the best time of her life and a little bubble of fear bounced around in her stomach that she'd never be happy again. In tribute to Eric, she had worn the Aquarium t-shirt he'd given her the day they met. She was thrilled it finally fit but it was also the only thing she could think of to do to let him know she'd never forget him.

Eric gave everyone hugs. He tousled the twin's hair and told them to stay out of trouble. Nicole thanked him continuously for playing for her at her birthday. Even the dogs ran around his feet until he picked them up and rubbed their bellies in one final gesture of love.

"I have something for you." He said and picked up a gift bag from off the grass by his feet when it was finally time for Daphne's turn to say goodbye.

Eagerly she pulled out the contents. Inside were several framed pictures of their time together; a framed picture of him with Nicole and Daphne in front of Cinderella's castle at Disneyland and one of him with her on the set of the video. There was one of her on the day he showed up outside in the limo, her face red and distorted in excitement.

"I hadn't even seen this ever." She said to Holly who grinned and shrugged her shoulders.

She hadn't expected him to do anything for her, but she pulled out something even more special than she could have imagined. It was a plaque engraved with the words of a song called, "How Could It Be" which was the song inspired by their conversation when he had first arrived.

"It's going to be one of the first singles we release from our next album, the word is that it will be a hit. My manager thinks it could even be a Grammy nominated song, so thanks to you too, for all you've done for me Daphne."

They shared a special hug, and as he headed out the door he promised to send everyone backstage passes for their shows.

"Aren't you going to walk him to the car?" Nicole whispered.

"No, this has been hard enough without watching him drive away." She said and hugged her friend.

At the doorway he looked and gave Daphne one final wink. She felt like her arm was being ripped off and cried some more as she held onto Nicole.

"Ok then." Nicole said as she waved to the limousine as it drove off and they watched it drive down the street until it turned onto the next street and was out of sight. They headed to the kitchen to make some lemonade and sit in the backyard.

In silence they sat, each contemplating their individual thoughts.

"So what do you think your mom is going to think when she gets home?" Nicole asked.

"I have no idea. I just hope she's happy. I hope she's happy for me." Daphne said. "She'll be in tomorrow but she said she wanted to give us one more day, so that she can get the house in order before we get there. And then that's it. I'm back home, and although things are completely different I'm sure in no time at all it'll be like a dream that I didn't really have."

"Daph, you know what, that's not how it's going to happen. You look different, you act different, you even have a different future now. You'll be designing scarves, you're going to have money in an account set aside for you to go to college, you'll have a car when you're sixteen, you know someone famous, and you're related to someone famous. You have new relationships, trust me, your life will not be the same."

Daphne nodded knowing in her heart it was true. She just had to see her mom to make sure it would all be possible. Daphne desperately wanted her mom's support and approval. If her mom was unhappy, she would be too.

In the warm sun Nicole and Daphne talked about the hopes and fears they had as they entered high school. Nicole wanted to join the literary magazine, newspaper and the yearbook, and Daphne hoped there would be some kind of crafts club she could join.

"Nicole, what about your other friends. They were really mean to me." Daphne said.

"Daphne, don't worry about them. Did I hang out with them at all this summer? It might be a little weird at first, but it's you and me okay?"

"I wonder what Eric is doing?"

Nicole laughed and threw an ice cube at her, "He's on a plane you dork."

With the exception of Eric leaving, the last day at her dad's house was like it was any other day. She hung out with Nicole and went to dinner with her dad and Holly and the younger kids. The day didn't feel as much like an ending as it did a transition. Daphne didn't know why she thought it'd be so traumatizing to leave, they lived in the same town and she could visit anytime like Holly said. She knew the days would run into the next the way they did before, maybe with a little bit more excitement this time. When Todd was driving them home, the boys chatted as usual and Daphne watched the scenery go by. She hadn't spoken to her mom since the conversation about the kidnapping episode. Daphne rolled her eyes even as she thought about it and they pulled in front of the house. She felt all the dread like always and didn't want to go in but knew she had too, even though her room would be different, and her life would be different.

When they walked in, the house was lit only by candles and Daphne was shocked to find that a lot of the furniture had been replaced.

"What happened here?" she asked as she turned to her dad.

"Mom! Mommy!" The boys shouted as they ran around looking for her mom.

She could hear her mom's happy voice and waited for her to come into the living room. Todd had gone back out to the car to bring in their bags. When Helen walked into the room, Daphne's jaw dropped. It was like looking into a mirror of transformation and she could barely contain her excitement.

"What happened to you?" Daphne exclaimed.

"Look at my baby girl!" Helen gushed and they rushed over to each other and looked each other up and down.

"Mom..." Daphne said.

"Well honey, I think the vacation was exactly what the doctor ordered. What do you think?"

Daphne looked over her mom who'd lost weight herself and looked great in a pair of capris and tank top. Her dark blonde hair had been trimmed and lightened and Daphne noted that her mom looked a lot like Helen Hunt.

"And what's with the furniture?" Daphne looked around.

"Helen, you look fantastic!" Todd said as he re-entered the house. "You met someone didn't you?"

Daphne watched her mother look down and smile.

"Mom, you met someone?" Daphne sat on the couch waiting for the details.

"Well, yes I did. He's coming for dinner tomorrow." She smiled and looked at Todd. "Thank you so much Todd. Taking the kids for the summer, getting away was exactly what I needed. I feel like a new woman and I owe you an apology." Helen frowned as she looked at Todd.

"Listen, we'll talk. We'll get through all of it." Todd said and reached for her mom and hugged her. Daphne hadn't seen her parents talk, let alone hug in years. She couldn't help but cry with happiness as she witnessed the possibility that her parents might be able to be friends again.

Todd walked out and the boys sat in front of the TV playing video games. Daphne and Helen sat on the couch sharing popcorn talking about their vacations. Helen was a little sorry that she wasn't able to be the one to take her to Disneyland, but was thrilled she was able to see it. Helen looked at all the pictures of Eric in disbelief still marveling over the fact that he was Holly's brother. Helen was in complete support of Daphne being a "freelance" designer for an accessories company that sold products to Fred Segal.

"That way I can send those designs and patterns and it won't interfere with school. Dad even set it up so that the paychecks will go directly to a trust fund until I go to college." Daphne was excited to share her plans with her mom.

"Your dad is a very smart man. He always was." Helen said as she put her arm around Daphne and held her close. Daphne soaked up the warmth from her mom; they never hung out and talked together. Daphne hoped it would be an everyday habit and not just a special occasion because they hadn't seen each other all summer.

"Daph, honey, I owe you an apology." Helen said.

Daphne felt a little nervous and looked to see the sincerity in her mom's face.

"I, I fell into a depression after the divorce and I hadn't realized how bad it was until I got away. I'm sorry for not being there for you, and not being more of a mom, but I didn't even know how bad it was. I kind of got stuck in time. I'm going to be okay though. I hate to say it took a man to get me out of my funk, but it did. I was feeling a little better about myself and Lou came around and was nice and kind and generous and made me feel good again. Let's just say that the time I spent with him reminded me that I could have fun again. And being attractive to a man was good because when your father left I thought that was it for me. It wasn't. Whatever ends up happening with me and Lou I promise you that I've seen the error of my ways and we'll never go there again. Ok?" Helen looked at Daphne hopefully.

"That's all I want to hear mom. I love you."

"I love you too sweetie."

Daphne was scared to bring it up, but she had to ask, "what about Holly? I really like her, and she really helped change my life mom. I mean, I love her." She looked down, dreading what her mom might have to say.

"Well, I know she did a lot of wonderful things for you kids this summer. I'm sorry for how I wronged you kids and kept you kids from them. We still need to work some things out but I know we can fix it."

There was a knock on the door and the boys ran to answer it.

Daphne could hear a loud voice that sounded familiar but she couldn't quite place it.

The boys came in followed by a short man, carrying flowers.

"What are you doing here a day early?" Helen asked, the smile overtaking her face so brightly it was like the light of a full moon on a dark night.

"I couldn't WAIT to see you." He said and handed her blushing mom the flowers.

"Director Lou!" Daphne laughed. "How in the world do you know my mom?"

"Hey KID! This is your mom?" he said and planted a kiss on Helen's cheek.

"How do you know Daphne?" Helen asked as she looked adoringly at the director.

"When I left Spain IT was to come to the STATES to shoot the video for Aquarium, remember." He said.

Daphne was in shock over what a small world it was.

"I'll put these in some water." Helen said, "I have some chicken if you're hungry sweetie."

Sweetie? Daphne thought to herself. She was very eager to see how this all happened but the phone rang and it was Nicole. Hands down she had to gossip with Nicole about her mom's new boyfriend, new look and the possibility that it would indeed all fall into place.

For the first day of high school Nicole and Daphne had agreed to meet in front of their new school. Daphne was expecting Nicole to be there with her friends from the previous year but Nicole was sitting on the brick wall in front of the office, her backpack by her feet eating a bagel.

"Oh my gosh. The day we'd been waiting for." Daphne said as she stood in front of her friend.

"Cool outfit," Nicole said between bites of bagel. Daphne

wore a tie dyed blue t-shirt that she stenciled the word Aquarium onto. Her signature by Daphne scarf was wrapped around her neck and she wore low hip hugger jeans, because now she could. After losing a total of 45 pounds over the summer, Daphne had more fun than she'd ever had shopping for new school clothes. She wore her favorite flip flops and her hair in a ponytail. She was not interested in getting dolled up and making everyone think she wanted to be popular. She'd had a taste of true fame and scandal with her picture being in the paper, the last thing she wanted was the kids who were so mean to her a few short months before trying to be her friend now.

Nicole, looked stylish and fabulous as always wearing a cotton mini skirt and a short coverlet sweater Daphne knit for her. She wore a tank top that had "…by daphne" stenciled on it and had her hair and makeup done. She looked like she stepped off the cover of a magazine.

"So, you ready to slay some senior hearts?" Nicole said as she jumped off the brick wall. Daphne shook her head and they walked towards the hall. High school was definitely going to be a blast. Her classes were mixed with so many new kids that she didn't have one class with any of the kids that harassed her from middle school. It was such a rush between classes that she didn't even see the mean ones. But some of the kids she did know would wave to her in passing.

Daphne was also excited that she had a couple classes with kids from different grades in them. In her Spanish class there were sophomores and juniors and in her home economics class there were even some seniors.

She hadn't seen any cute boys that grabbed her attention. After a celebrity like Eric, or a college boy like Robert, she didn't really expect to "like" anyone. But cute guys would be fun anyway if she could find one.

At lunch Nicole and Daphne met to discuss their classes and the first club they would try to join. They were excited that the first assembly and dance had been scheduled for a couple weeks away after the first home game. Daphne hadn't attended any of the dances in middle school and was eager to see what the high school dances would be like.

Daphne and Nicole did have English together, the last period of the day which gave them plenty of time to plan what they would do for the evenings. They had already planned over the summer that every other weekend Nicole's mom would pick them up from school and Daphne would stay with her dad and spend the weekend.

They took their respective busses home and Daphne was excited to see her mom alone for an hour before her brothers got home from school.

Her mom taught college classes so she had a strange schedule. Some days she worked during the days and others she worked at night. Today was a night class and Daphne was excited to go home and tell her mom about her day.

When she walked through the door she was happy to find a juice and a bowl of grapes set out on the table. It was the after school snack her mom used to have ready for them years ago before her parents separated. She'd stopped doing that for them a long time before.

Daphne set down the hobo bag she made to put her books in instead of having to carry a backpack like everyone else, and waited for her mom to join her. Daphne loved the crunchiness of the grapes as her mom entered with a big smile on her face.

"Well how was it?" Helen asked. Daphne told her all about how fun her classes were and how the kids seemed a lot less interested in her and picking on her the way they were the previous year.

"That's great Daphne. High school can be a lot of fun." Helen said.

"Yeah mom, I can tell I'm really going to like high school."

Helen took Daphne's hand in her hand and held it while Daphne munched on more grapes.

"You've certainly come a long way. From begging me to home school you, to saying you're going to like high school what a relief Daphne."

Daphne smiled to herself. She had come a long way. She'd started the summer miserable, bitter and sad. Now she started a new chapter in her life, hopeful, excited and happy and knew that she had a support system, and love, and nothing could stop her now.

Her daydreams had become her reality, and she eagerly awaited what life would hand her next.